Agatha Christie

Agatha Christie (1890-1976) is known throughout the world as the Queen of Crime. Her books have sold over a billion copies in English with another billion in over 100 foreign languages. She is the most widely published and translated author of all time and in any language; only the Bible and Shakespeare have sold more copies. She is the author of 80 crime novels and short story collections, 19 plays, and six other novels. *The Mousetrap*, her most famous play, was first staged in 1952 in London and is still performed there – it is the longest-running play in history.

Agatha Christie's first novel was published in 1920. It featured Hercule Poirot, the Belgian detective who has become the most popular detective in crime fiction since Sherlock Holmes. Collins has published Agatha Christie since 1926.

This series has been especially created for readers worldwide whose first language is not English. Each story has been shortened, and the vocabulary and grammar simplified to make it accessible to readers with a good intermediate knowledge of the language.

The following features are included after the story:

A **List of characters** to help the reader identify who is who, and how they are connected to each other. **Cultural notes** to explain historical and other references. A **Glossary** of words that some readers may not be familiar with are explained. There is also a **Recording** of the story.

Agatha Christie

After the Funeral

Collins

HarperCollins Publishers
77–85 Fulham Palace Road
London W6 8JB

www.collinselt.com

Collins ® is a registered trademark of HarperCollins Publishers Limited.

This *Collins English Readers* edition published 2012

Reprint 10 9 8 7 6 5 4 3 2 1 0

First published in Great Britain by Collins 1953

AGATHA CHRISTIE™ POIROT™ After the Funeral™
Copyright © 1953 Agatha Christie Limited. All rights reserved.
Copyright © 2012 After the Funeral™ abridged edition
Agatha Christie Limited. All rights reserved.
www.agathachristie.com

ISBN: 978-0-00-745169-2

A catalogue record for this book is available from the British Library.

Cover by crushed.co.uk © HarperCollins/Agatha Christie Ltd 2008

Typeset by Aptara in India.

Printed and bound in Great Britain by Clays Ltd, St Ives plc.

Contents

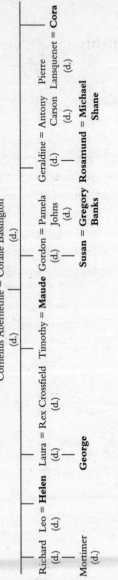

Abernethie Family Tree

Cornelius Abernethie = Coralie Bassington
(d.)

Richard	Leo = **Helen**	Laura = Rex Crossfield	Timothy = **Maude**
(d.)	(d.)	(d.)	

Mortimer
(d.)

George

Gordon = Pamela Johns
(d.) (d.)

Susan = **Gregory Banks**

Geraldine = Antony Carson
(d.) (d.)

Pierre Lansquenet = **Cora**
(d.)

Rosamund = **Michael Shane**

Key

= married

(d.) died

The people whose names are in **bold** were present at the funeral of Richard Abernethie

Chapter 1

Old Lanscombe, the <u>butler</u> at Enderby Hall, shook his head. Soon they would be coming back from his <u>Master's</u> <u>funeral</u>. Mr Richard Abernethie had been a good employer. He had died very suddenly, aged sixty-eight. Although he was ill, the family doctor thought that he would live for another two years. Ah, but the Master had never recovered from his son's death, six months before. Mortimer Abernethie's death was a huge shock because he was such a strong and healthy young man.

Mr Richard was twenty-four when his father, Cornelius, died, and he had gone straight into the family business. He ran it successfully while keeping a very happy home in this huge <u>Victorian</u> house. He was like a father to his younger brothers and sisters. Now Leo, Laura, Geraldine, and Gordon were dead, only Timothy and Cora were left. It had been twenty-five years since Lanscombe had seen Cora, and he hadn't recognized her when she arrived before the funeral. She had grown so fat – and was dressed in a loose black dress with too many black necklaces! Well, Miss Cora had always been a bit – well, *strange*.

She had remembered *him* all right. 'Why, it's Lanscombe!' she had said, and seemed so pleased to see him. Ah, they had all been fond of him in the old days.

Now cars were arriving, bringing the family home, and Lanscombe showed them all into the green sitting room.

A few minutes later, standing in front of the fireplace, Mr Entwhistle, the family lawyer, looked round. He did not know all the people there very well – some he had only met before the funeral and he needed to sort them out in his mind before he read the <u>will</u>. When he saw old Lanscombe handing round drinks, Mr Entwhistle thought, 'Poor old man – he's nearly ninety, and half blind. Well, he'll have that nice little <u>inheritance</u> from Richard.'

Leo Abernethie's <u>widow</u>, Helen, he knew well. She was a very charming woman of fifty-one. It was strange that she had never married again after Leo's death, he thought.

Mr Entwhistle moved his attention on to George Crossfield, Laura Abernethie's son. Laura had left very little money when she died five years ago. George was a lawyer and a handsome young man – but there was a dishonest feel about him.

Now which of the two young women was which? Ah yes, that was Rosamund, Geraldine's daughter, looking at the wax flowers on the green marble table. She was a beautiful girl, but silly. She was an actress, not a very good one, and she had married an actor, Michael Shane, fair-haired and handsome. *And* he knows he is, thought Mr Entwhistle.

Susan, the <u>late</u> Gordon Abernethie's daughter, would be much better on the stage than Rosamund, Mr Entwhistle thought – she had far more personality. She also had dark hair and eyes that were almost golden in colour. Beside her was Gregory Banks, the man she had just married. He was a pharmacist's assistant! In Mr Entwhistle's world, girls did not marry men who worked in a shop. The young man, who had a pale face, seemed uncomfortable.

His eyes went on to Mrs Maude Abernethie. A big, sensible woman, she had always been a good wife to Timothy, who had been an <u>invalid</u> for many years. Mr Entwhistle <u>suspected</u> that Timothy only imagined that he was ill, that he was a <u>hypochondriac</u>, in fact.

Then Mr Entwhistle looked next at Cora Lansquenet. Her mother had died giving birth to her. Poor little Cora! She was an <u>awkward</u> girl, always saying the wrong thing. She met Pierre

Lansquenet, who was half French, at art school. At the time, Cora's brother, Richard Abernethie, suspected that Lansquenet was looking for a rich wife, but Cora, who was not rich, ran away and married him anyway. They spent most of their married life in seaside towns that other painters seemed to live in, as well.

Lansquenet was a very bad painter, but Richard had generously given his young sister an <u>income</u>. Lansquenet had died twelve years ago, and now here was his widow, back in the home of her childhood, exclaiming with pleasure whenever she recalled some childish memory.

Chapter 2

'As you know,' said Mr Entwhistle, 'I am the <u>executor</u> of Richard Abernethie's will . . .'

'*I* didn't know,' interrupted Cora Lansquenet. 'Did he leave me anything?'

Ignoring her, Entwhistle continued, 'Originally, Richard Abernethie's will left almost everything to his son Mortimer. After Mortimer's death, Richard decided to get to know his nephew and nieces better before he made a new will.'

'Did he leave *me* anything?' repeated Cora.

Mr Entwhistle again ignored her, 'Apart from a <u>legacy</u> to Lanscombe, everything Richard owned is going to be divided into six equal parts. Four of these will go to: Richard's brother Timothy; his nephew George Crossfield; and his nieces Susan Banks and Rosamund Shane. The other two parts are going to be <u>invested</u> and the income from them will be paid to Mrs Helen Abernethie, the widow of his brother Leo; and to his sister, Mrs Cora Lansquenet. After their death the money is to be divided between the other four <u>beneficiaries</u> or their children.'

'That's *very* nice!' said Cora Lansquenet. 'How much?'

'About three to four thousand pounds a year.'

'Good!' said Cora. 'I shall go and visit Italy.'

Helen Abernethie said softly, 'How generous of Richard.'

'He was very fond of you,' said Mr Entwhistle.

Helen said regretfully, 'I wish I had realised how ill he was.'

'Nobody expected Richard to die as soon as he did. Even the doctor was surprised,' said Mr Entwhistle.

'"*Suddenly, at his <u>residence</u>*" it said in the newspaper,' said Cora. 'I wondered then . . . Still, it's been kept quiet very nicely, hasn't it? I think you're all right. I mean – it should be kept in the family.'

The faces that had turned towards her looked amazed.

Mr Entwhistle said, 'Really, Cora, I'm afraid I don't understand what you mean.'

Cora Lansquenet looked round in surprise. 'But he *was* murdered, wasn't he?' she said.

Chapter 3

As he returned south to London by train, Mr Entwhistle thought about what Cora had said, and how everyone had reacted.

Maude had exclaimed, '*Really*, Cora!'

Somebody else had said, 'What *do* you mean?'

And at once Cora had said, 'Oh, I didn't mean – oh, but I did think from what he said – and his death was so sudden! Oh, please forget that I said anything at all – I know I'm always saying the wrong thing.'

And then there had been a discussion about Richard Abernethie's personal belongings. The house and its contents, Mr Entwhistle said, would be sold.

Cora's unfortunate comment had been forgotten. After all, Cora had always been, if not subnormal, embarrassingly <u>naïve</u>. She had always said unwelcome truths.

Mr Entwhistle's thoughts stopped there. Yes, it was because Cora's comments were true, that they were so embarrassing!

When Mr Entwhistle had looked at Cora earlier, she had not *looked* like the girl he had known. But Cora's <u>mannerisms</u> were still there – such as the way she <u>tilted</u> her head to one side as she spoke. He remembered two phrases now.

'But I did think from what he said . . .' and 'His death was so sudden.'

Yes, Richard's death had been sudden. Richard's doctor had said only months ago that if Richard looked after himself, he might live two or three years. Perhaps longer.

Well, doctors could never be sure about how each patient would react to a disease. And Richard Abernethie had no great wish to live after his son Mortimer's death because there was no child or grandchild of his to <u>inherit</u> his <u>fortune</u> and his business.

During the last six months, Richard, who had obviously been searching for an <u>heir</u>, had invited to stay with him, at different times, his nephew George, his niece Susan and her husband, and his niece Rosamund and her husband. Richard had also briefly visited his hypochondriac brother, Timothy.

The will that Richard had eventually made told Mr Entwhistle how disappointed he was with all of them.

Mr Entwhistle remembered what Cora had said earlier that day, 'I did think from what he *said* . . .'

He asked himself, What *did* Richard say? And *when* did he say it? Did Richard visit Cora Lansquenet or was it something he wrote in a letter to her which made her ask that shocking question:

'But he *was* murdered, wasn't he?'

* * *

Further along the train, Gregory Banks said to his wife, Susan, 'That aunt of yours must be completely mad!'

'Aunt Cora? Oh, yes.'

George Crossfield said <u>sharply,</u> 'She really shouldn't say things like that. It might put ideas into people's heads.'

Rosamund's husband, Michael, said, 'I think George is right. It's so easy to start people talking.'

'Well, would it matter? It might be fun,' said Rosamund.

'Fun?' Four voices spoke at once.

'Having a murder in the family,' said Rosamund. 'And if he *was* murdered, who do you think did it? His death has been very convenient for *all* of us. Michael and I are completely <u>broke</u>. Michael was offered a really good part in a play if he could afford to wait for it, but he couldn't. Now we'll have enough money for our *own* play if we want to.'

Nobody was listening. They were thinking about their own futures.

'Now I can put my <u>clients</u>' money back in their accounts before they notice it's missing,' thought George.

Gregory thought, 'Now I can escape from this prison I'm in.'

Susan's hard, young eyes softened as she looked at her husband. She suspected that Greg loved her less than she loved him – but that only strengthened her feelings. Greg was hers; she would do anything for him. Anything.

★ ★ ★

Maude Abernethie, who was staying the night at Enderby, wondered if she should offer to stay longer to help Helen with the clearing of the house. But she really had to get back to Timothy to look after him. He had expected that most of Richard's fortune would come to *him* and he would be annoyed – and that was so bad for his health.

She sighed, then smiled. Things were going to be much easier now, financially. They could spend money on plants for the garden, for instance.

★ ★ ★

Helen Abernethie sat by the fire in the sitting room at Enderby Hall. How worried she had been lately about money. Now, thanks to Richard, all that was over.

Helen looked at the bouquet of wax flowers that stood on the green marble table. Cora had been sitting beside it when they had been waiting to go to the funeral. She had been so pleased at being back in her old home. Oh, but the way Cora had asked, 'But he *was* murdered, wasn't he?'

The faces all round, shocked, staring at her!

And suddenly, seeing the picture of everyone clearly in her mind, Helen <u>frowned</u>. There was something wrong with that picture. Was it an expression on someone's face? Was that it? Something that should not have been there ?

No, she didn't know what it was – but there had been something, somewhere, that was *wrong*.

* * *

Meanwhile, in the café at Swindon Railway Station, a lady in black was waiting for the connecting train to Lytchett St Mary, where she lived. She was eating cakes and looking forward to the future.

All those faces – when she had said that about murder! Well, it had been the right thing to say.

She smiled like a happy child. She was really going to enjoy herself at last.

Chapter 4

At a quarter to six the next evening Mr Entwhistle's telephone rang. The caller informed him that Mrs Cora Lansquenet had been murdered in her cottage in the village of Lytchett St Mary.

★ ★ ★

The next day a police <u>Inspector</u> named Morton came to see him and said, 'It's not a very easy <u>case</u>, Mr Entwhistle. Let's imagine someone was watching Cora Lansquenet's house and saw her <u>companion</u>, Miss Gilchrist, come out of the house at about two o'clock. This someone then <u>deliberately</u> takes the <u>hatchet</u> that was lying by the woodshed, smashes the kitchen window, gets into the house, goes upstairs, and attacks Mrs Lansquenet. She was hit six or eight times – it was a very violent crime. Then he opens a few cupboards, picks up a few pieces of cheap jewellery, and makes his escape.'

'She was in bed?'

'Yes. She returned late from the North the night before and woke with a terrible headache. She took some painkillers but felt no better by lunchtime. She decided to take two sleeping pills and sent Miss Gilchrist into town to change some library books. When this man broke in he could have taken what he wanted just by <u>threatening</u> her. Why did he need to kill her? It looks like she was sleeping peacefully when she was attacked.'

'We do hear of pointless murders,' Mr Entwhistle said.

'Oh yes, that's why we're looking for any <u>suspicious</u> stranger who was seen in the neighbourhood: the local people all have <u>alibis</u>. Of course, her cottage is up a little road outside the village. Anyone could get there without being seen. There has been no rain for some days, so there aren't any car tracks to go by – in case anyone came by car.

'There are strange things about the case, Mr Entwhistle. These, for instance.' Inspector Morton pushed across his desk a collection of cheap jewellery. 'Those are the things that were taken. They were found just outside the house, hidden in a bush.

'Of course the companion, Miss Gilchrist, may have killed Miss Lansquenet, but I doubt it. Everyone says they were very friendly.' He paused before continuing, 'According to you, nobody gains from Mrs Lansquenet's death.'

'I didn't say that,' replied Mr Entwhistle. 'Mrs Lansquenet's income was an <u>allowance</u> made to her by her brother, her house is rented, and the furniture and jewellery would not be worth much to whoever she's left it to. However, her legacy from her brother will be divided amongst the five other beneficiaries of Richard Abernethie's will, so all of them will benefit from her death.'

The Inspector looked disappointed. 'Well, there doesn't seem to be a strong <u>motive</u> there for anyone to kill her – and especially not with a hatchet. You'll be going to see Miss Gilchrist, I suppose? She's told us, I think, everything that she can, but you never know. Sometimes, in conversation, people remember things. She's a sensible woman – and she's really been most helpful.'

Strange, thought Mr Entwhistle, that Cora had been thinking about murder the very day before she herself was murdered.

'He *was* murdered, wasn't he?'

It was too <u>ridiculous</u> to mention to Inspector Morton. But what if Miss Gilchrist could tell him what Richard had said to Cora? I must see Miss Gilchrist immediately, said Mr Entwhistle to himself.

★ ★ ★

Miss Gilchrist was a thin woman with short, grey hair. 'I'm *so* pleased you have come, Mr Entwhistle,' she said. 'I've never, ever had any involvement with a *murder*. You *read* about them, of course, but I don't even really like doing *that*.'

Following her into the sitting room, Mr Entwhistle looked around him. There was a strong smell of oil paint and the cottage walls were covered with mostly very dark and dirty oil paintings. But there were watercolour paintings as well, and smaller pictures were in a pile on the window seat.

'Mrs Lansquenet used to buy paintings at sales,' Miss Gilchrist explained. 'She never paid more than a pound for any of them, and there was a wonderful chance, she always said, of finding something valuable.'

Entwhistle doubted if any of these were worth even the pound she had paid for them!

'Of course,' said Miss Gilchrist, noticing his expression, 'I don't know much myself, though my father was a painter – not a very successful one. But I used to do watercolours myself as a girl and it was nice for Mrs Lansquenet to have someone she could talk to about painting and who would understand.'

'You were fond of her?'

'Oh *yes*,' said Miss Gilchrist. 'In some ways, Mrs Lansquenet was just like a child. She said anything that came into her head – but it surprised me sometimes how accurate she could be about things other than art.'

'You were with Mrs Lansquenet for some years?'

'Three and a half. I did most of the cooking – I enjoy cooking – and some light housework. None of the *rough* housework, of course. Mrs Panter came in for that. I could not possibly have been a *servant*. I used to have a little tearoom: The Willow Tree – it was a lovely place. All the cups and plates were blue and the cakes were *really* good. I was doing well and then the war came and food supplies were cut and I had to close the tearoom and had no money to pay the rent. And so I had to look round for something to do, but, I had never been trained for anything. I went to work for one lady as her companion, but she was so rude – and then I came to Mrs Lansquenet and we were friends from the start.' Miss Gilchrist added sadly, 'How I loved my dear, dear little tearoom. Such *nice* people used to come to it!

'But I must not talk about myself. The police have been very kind. Inspector Morton even arranged for me to spend the night with someone in the village, but I felt it was my duty to stay here with all Mrs Lansquenet's nice things in the house. The Inspector told me there would be a policeman on duty in the kitchen all night – because of the broken window – it was fixed this morning – though to be honest, I *did* pull the dressing table across the door . . .'

Mr Entwhistle said quickly, 'I know the main facts, but if it would not upset you too much to give me your own story of what happened . . .?'

'Of course.'

'Mrs Lansquenet got back from the funeral the night before last,' Mr Entwhistle said. 'Did she talk about the funeral at all?'

'Just a little. I gave her a cup of hot milk and she told me that the church had been full and that she was sorry she hadn't seen her other brother – Timothy. Well, then she said she would go to bed.'

'She said nothing else that you can remember specially?'

'She asked me if I would like to go to Italy. Italy! Of course I said it would be wonderful – and she said, "We'll go!" She told me that her brother had left her a very good income. Poor dear. Well, I'm glad she had the pleasure of planning.' Miss Gilchrist sighed, 'I don't suppose I shall ever go to Italy now . . .'

'And the next morning?' Mr Entwhistle asked.

'The next morning Mrs Lansquenet wasn't at all well. She'd had almost no sleep at all, she told me, because of bad dreams. She had her breakfast in bed, and at lunchtime she told me that she still hadn't been able to sleep. "I keep thinking of things and wondering," she said. And then she said that she would take some sleeping tablets and try and get a good sleep in the afternoon. She wanted me to go into town and change her library books. So I left just after two and that – and that – was the last time . . .' Miss Gilchrist began to cry. 'She must have been asleep, you know, and the Inspector says that she didn't feel anything . . . And do tell her relations that apart from having such a bad night, she was really very happy and looking forward to the future.'

'She did not speak at all about her brother's death? The – er – cause of it?'

'No. He had been ill for some time,' said Miss Gilchrist, 'though I was surprised to hear it. He looked so very full of life.'

Mr Entwhistle said quickly, 'You saw him? When?'

'About three weeks ago. It was a surprise. Mrs Lansquenet hadn't expected him. It upset her. She said something like "Poor Richard. He sounds <u>senile</u>. All these silly ideas that someone is poisoning him. Old people get like that." And of course, that is only too *true*. When my aunt got old, she thought the servants were trying to poison *her*!'

Mr Entwhistle was very worried. Richard Abernethie had *not* been senile. He asked whether Miss Gilchrist knew if Cora Lansquenet had left a will. She replied that Mrs Lansquenet's will was at the bank.

With that he left. He insisted on Miss Gilchrist accepting some money for her <u>expenses</u> and told her he would contact her again. In the meantime he would be grateful if she would stay on at the cottage while she looked for a new job.

Mr Entwhistle then left to talk to the bank manager and to have a further conversation with Inspector Morton.

Chapter 5

That evening, the phone rang and Mr Entwhistle heard Maude Abernethie's voice. 'Thank goodness you're there! This news about Cora has upset Timothy <u>dreadfully</u> – was it really murder?'

'Yes,' said Mr Entwhistle.

'It seems incredible,' said Maude. 'And I am *very* worried about Timothy. It's so bad for him, all this. He insists that you come up here to Yorkshire and see him. He wants to know if Cora left a will.'

'There is a will. She left instructions for Timothy to be her executor but I will arrange everything. She left her own paintings and a piece of jewellery to her companion, Miss Gilchrist, and everything else to her niece, Susan.'

'To Susan? But why Susan?'

'Perhaps because she thought Susan had made a marriage that the family disapproved of. When all the bills are paid and the furniture is sold, I doubt Susan will get more than five hundred pounds. The <u>inquest</u> will be next Thursday. I will need Timothy's signature on certain documents as he is the executor, so I think it might be a good thing if I did come and see you.'

'That is wonderful! Tomorrow? And you'll stay the night? The best train is the 11.20 from St Pancras.'

'I will have to take an afternoon train, I'm afraid. I have other business in the morning.'

Mr Entwhistle's 'other business' was visiting George, Rosamund and Susan.

★ ★ ★

Mr Entwhistle said, 'I tried to phone you the day after the funeral, but you weren't in the office.'

'They never told me,' said George Crossfield. 'I thought I should have a day off after the good news!'

'The good news?'

George's face went red.

'Oh, I didn't mean Uncle Richard's *death*. But knowing you've inherited money certainly makes you feel lucky, so I went to the <u>horse-races</u> at Hurst Park. And I <u>placed bets</u> on two horses that won. I only made fifty pounds, but it all helps pay the bills.'

'Oh yes,' said Mr Entwhistle. 'And there will now be additional money coming to you as a result of your Aunt Cora's death.'

'Poor old girl,' George said. 'It does seem bad luck, doesn't it? I expect the police will question all the strange characters in the neighbourhood and make them <u>prove</u> where they were when the murder happened.'

'Not so easy if a little time has passed,' said Mr Entwhistle. 'I was in a bookshop at half past three on that day. But would I remember that if I was questioned in ten days' time? Would *you* remember which day you went to the races in – say – a month's time?'

'Oh, I would remember because it was the day after the funeral.'

'True – true. And then you bet on two winning horses. You wouldn't forget that! Which were they, by the way?'

'Gaymarck and Frogg II. Yes, I won't forget them in a hurry.'

Mr Entwhistle gave a small laugh and left.

★ ★ ★

'It's lovely to see you,' said Rosamund, 'but it's very early in the morning.'

'It's eleven o'clock!' said Mr Entwhistle.

Michael Shane appeared, yawning.

The lawyer did not approve of the young Shanes' way of living. He disliked the bottles and glasses that lay about the sitting room and the untidiness of it all.

But Rosamund and Michael were certainly a very handsome couple and they seemed very fond of each other.

Mr Entwhistle said, 'I have just come back from Lytchett St Mary.'

'Then it *was* Aunt Cora who was murdered?' Rosamund said. 'We saw it in the newspaper. And I said it must be. Two murders, one after another!'

'Don't be silly, Rosamund,' said Michael. 'Your Uncle Richard wasn't murdered.'

'Well, Cora thought he was.'

Mr Entwhistle interrupted. 'You did come back to London after the funeral, didn't you? I ask because I phoned you the following day – several times in fact, and couldn't get an answer.'

'Oh dear. We were here until about twelve, and then Michael went to lunch with someone. I had a lovely afternoon shopping – and then we had dinner at a Spanish restaurant. We got back here about ten o'clock that night, I suppose.'

Michael was looking thoughtfully at Mr Entwhistle. 'What did you want to ask us, Sir?'

'Oh! Just some things about Richard Abernethie's <u>estate</u>.'

Rosamund asked, 'Do we get the money now, or not for a long time?'

'I'm afraid,' said Mr Entwhistle, 'that the law is full of delays.'

'But we can get some money in advance, can't we?' Rosamund looked worried. 'It's very important. Because of the play.'

Michael said pleasantly, 'Oh, there's no real hurry. It's just a question of deciding whether to finance the play or not.'

'It will be very easy to advance you some money,' said Mr Entwhistle.

'Then that's all right.' Rosamund gave a sigh of relief. 'Did Aunt Cora leave any money?'

'A little. She left it to your cousin Susan.'

'Why Susan? Is it much?'

'A few hundred pounds and some furniture.'

'Nice furniture?'

'No,' said Mr Entwhistle.

Rosamund lost interest. 'It's all very strange, isn't it?' she said. 'There was Cora, after the funeral, suddenly saying, "He *was* murdered!" and then, the very next day, *she* is murdered? I mean, it *is* strange, isn't it?'

Mr Entwhistle said quietly, 'Yes, it is very strange.'

★ ★ ★

Mr Entwhistle studied Susan Banks as she talked. In many ways she reminded him of her uncle, Richard Abernethie. She had the same energy he had. And yet Richard Abernethie had left her no more than the others. The reason must be because he didn't like her husband.

Mr Entwhistle looked at Gregory Banks, a thin, pale young man with reddish hair. He was quite pleasant, and yet there was something about him that made Mr Entwhistle <u>uneasy</u>. What had attracted Susan to him? It was obvious that her world revolved around her husband.

'Have they any idea *at all* who the murderer might be?' Susan asked.

'They wouldn't tell me if they did – and the murder took place only the day before yesterday,' said Mr Entwhistle.

'It's definitely got to be a certain kind of person,' Susan was thoughtful. 'Someone violent, perhaps <u>insane</u> – I mean, to use a hatchet like that. But thinking of possible motives – did Cora leave her companion anything?'

'A small piece of jewellery of no great value and some watercolours of fishing villages of <u>sentimental</u> value only.'

'Well, no motive there – unless one is insane.'

Mr Entwhistle gave a little laugh. 'As far as I can see, the only person who had a motive is *you*, my dear Susan.'

'What's that?' An ugly light showed in Greg's eyes. 'How is Sue involved? What do you mean – saying things like that?'

'Just my little joke,' said Mr Entwhistle apologetically. 'Cora left her estate to you, Susan. But nobody can suggest than an estate of a few hundred pounds at the most is a motive for murder, for a young lady who has just inherited several hundred thousand pounds from her uncle.'

'She left her estate to me?' Susan sounded surprised. 'How extraordinary. She didn't even know me!'

'I think she had heard <u>rumours</u> that there had been a little difficulty – er – over your marriage. There had been a certain amount of trouble over her own marriage – and I think she felt you were alike.'

'She married an artist, didn't she? Was he a good artist?'

Mr Entwhistle shook his head.

'Are there any of his paintings in the cottage?'

'Yes.'

'Then I shall judge for myself,' said Susan. 'Is there anybody at the cottage now?'

'I have arranged for Miss Gilchrist to stay there,' Mr Entwhistle said. 'Your aunt made your Uncle Timothy her executor, so I will tell him of your decision to go down to the cottage. And what are your plans for the future?'

'I've got my eye on a building in Cardigan Street where I want to open a beauty salon. I suppose you can advance me some money? I may have to pay a deposit.'

'I can arrange that,' said Mr Entwhistle. 'I telephoned you the day after the funeral several times – but could get no answer. I thought perhaps you might like an advance. I wondered whether you might have gone out of town.'

'Oh no,' said Susan quickly. 'We were in all day.'

Greg said gently, 'You know Susan, I think our telephone wasn't working that day. I couldn't get through to someone I telephoned in the afternoon. I meant to report it, but it was all right the next morning.'

'Telephones,' said Mr Entwhistle, 'can be very unreliable sometimes.'

Susan said suddenly, 'How did Aunt Cora know about our marriage?'

'Richard may have told her. She changed her will about three weeks ago – just about the time he had been to see her.'

Susan looked surprised. 'Did Uncle Richard go to see her? I'd no idea! So that was when . . .'

'When what?'

'Nothing,' said Susan.

Chapter 6

'It's very good of you to come,' said Maude Abernethie, as she led Mr Entwhistle to a very old car. 'I'm sorry about this old thing. In fact, it broke down when I was coming back after the funeral. I had to walk a couple of miles to the nearest garage and stay at a small hotel while they fixed it and *that* upset Timothy. I try to keep things from him as much as possible – but some things I can't do anything about – Cora's murder, for instance. I had to ask Dr Barton to give him something to calm him down. It seems so strange for someone to break in and murder her in the middle of the afternoon. If you broke into a house, surely you'd do it at night – and there must have been times during the day when both Cora and her companion were out and the house was empty. It doesn't make sense to commit a murder unless it's absolutely necessary.'

Does murder ever make sense? It depended, Mr Entwhistle thought, on the mind of the murderer.

They arrived at a very large house which badly needed painting.

'We have no servants,' said Maude slightly angrily as she led the way in. 'Just a couple of women who come in every morning. If I have to go out in the afternoon, Timothy is completely alone.'

Maude led the way into the sitting room where she had already put tea things by the fireplace, and seating Mr Entwhistle there, disappeared. She returned in a few minutes' with a teapot and homemade cake.

Looking at Maude in the light of the fire, Mr Entwhistle suddenly felt sad. Maude Abernethie had not had any children but she was a woman built for motherhood. Her hypochondriac husband had become her child, to be guarded and watched over.

Poor Maude, thought Mr Entwhistle.

★ ★ ★

'It is good of you to come, Entwhistle.' Timothy raised himself up in his chair as he held out a hand. 'I mustn't do too much,' he said. 'The doctor's <u>forbidden</u> it. You'll have to do everything for me, Entwhistle. *I* can't go to the inquest or be bothered by business of any kind connected with Cora's estate. What happens to Cora's share of Richard's money? It comes to me, I suppose?'

Saying something about preparing dinner, Maude left the room.

'The sum left invested for Cora,' said Mr Entwhistle, 'goes equally to you and George, Rosamund and Susan.'

'But I'm her only surviving brother! I couldn't believe it when Maude came home and told me about Richard's will. I thought she'd made a mistake. She is the best woman in the world, Maude – but women don't understand money. I don't believe she even realises that if Richard hadn't died when he did, we might have had to leave our home here. That is a fact!'

'Surely if you had asked Richard . . .'

Timothy gave a short laugh. 'I did say once to Richard that this place was getting a bit expensive to run and he said that we would be much better off in a smaller place altogether. It would be easier for Maude, he said! Oh no, I wouldn't have asked Richard for help. But I can tell you, Entwhistle, that the worry affected my health badly. Then Richard died and I felt so relieved about the future. But what hurt me was how Richard left his money. I assumed that he would leave everything to *me*. He came here – not long after Mortimer's death – because he wanted to talk about the family. We discussed young George – and Rosamund and Susan and their husbands. Both of those girls have made bad marriages, if you ask me. Well, I thought Richard was asking for my advice because I would be head of the family after he died, and so I thought the control of the money would be mine.'

In his excitement Timothy had kicked aside the blanket that covered his legs and sat up straight in his chair. He looked, Mr Entwhistle thought, a perfectly healthy man.

'Will you have a drink, Entwhistle?'

'Not quite so soon. Maude has just given me an excellent tea.'

Timothy looked at him. 'She's a capable woman. Maude. She even fixes that old car of ours – she's a good mechanic in her way, you know.'

'Yes, I hear the car broke down coming back from the funeral. Timothy, I don't know how much Maude told you about the funeral and the relatives. Cora said that Richard had been murdered. Perhaps Maude told you.'

Timothy laughed. 'That's just the sort of thing Cora would say!'

Maude came into the room and said firmly, 'I think, Timothy dear, that Mr Entwhistle has been with you long enough. You really *must* rest. If you have arranged everything . . .'

'Oh, we've arranged things. I'll leave it all to you, Entwhistle. You'll see to Cora's funeral – won't you? We shan't be able to come, but send an expensive <u>wreath</u> from us.'

Mr Entwhistle left for London by the breakfast train the following morning.

When he got home, he telephoned a friend of his.

Chapter 7

'I can't tell you how pleased I am that you were able to see me so soon,' Mr Entwhistle said as Hercule Poirot led him to a chair by the fire. On one side of the room a table was laid for two.

Poirot said, 'You are welcome, _mon ami_. I returned from the country this morning. And you have something you wish to discuss with me?'

'Yes. It's a long story, I'm afraid.'

'Then we will not have it until after we have eaten. Georges?'

Poirot's manservant, Georges, came in immediately with some <u>pâté de foie gras</u> and hot toast.

'We will have our pâté by the fire,' said Poirot. 'Afterwards we will move to the table . . .'

It was an hour and a half later that Mr Entwhistle sighed happily. 'You certainly know how to eat well, Poirot.'

'At my age, the main pleasure, almost the _only_ pleasure that still remains, is the pleasure of the table,' the Belgian detective said.

A very good <u>port</u> was now by Mr Entwhistle's side. Poirot had a sweet liqueur.

'I don't know,' said Mr Entwhistle, 'whether I'm making a fool of myself. But I'm going to put the facts before you, and then I'd like to know what you think.'

He paused for a moment or two, then he started speaking again. He told the story clearly, which was appreciated by the little man with the egg-shaped head who sat listening to him.

When Entwhistle had finished there was a pause. Then Hercule Poirot said at last, 'It seems very clear. You have in your mind the suspicion that your friend, Richard Abernethie may have been murdered? A suspicion that you made on the basis of one thing only – *the words spoken by Cora Lansquenet at Richard Abernethie's funeral*. The fact that she herself was murdered the day afterwards may be a <u>coincidence</u>. It is true that Richard Abernethie died suddenly, but he was being seen by a doctor who had no suspicions. Was Richard <u>buried</u> or <u>cremated</u>?'

'Cremated – at his own request.'

'So we come back to the essential point: *what Cora Lansquenet said*. And the real point is – that you believe she was speaking the truth.'

'Yes, I do,' replied Mr Entwhistle

'Why? Is it because already you had an uneasiness about the way Richard's death happened?'

The lawyer shook his head. 'No, no, it isn't that.'

'Then it is because of *her* – of Cora herself. You knew her well?'

'I had not seen her for – oh – over thirty years.'

'Would you have known her if you had met her in the street?'

Mr Entwhistle thought hard. 'I might have passed her by in the street without recognising her. But the moment I spoke to her face to face I would have recognised her. She wore her hair in the same way, and had a trick of looking up at you through her <u>fringe</u>, and she had a way of putting her head on one side and then suddenly saying something shocking. She had *character*, you see and character is always highly individual.'

'She was, in fact, the same Cora you had known years ago. And she still said shocking things!' said Poirot. 'The shocking things she had said in the past – were they usually correct?'

'That was always the awkward thing about Cora. She spoke the truth when it would have been better not to.'

'And Cora was quite sure Richard had been murdered. So *she must have had some reason for the belief*. Now tell me – when she said what she did, everyone <u>protested</u> immediately – that is right? And she then became confused and said something like "But I thought – from what he told me . . ."'

The lawyer nodded. 'I wish I could remember more clearly. But I'm fairly sure she used the words "he told me" or "he said . . ."'

'And then everyone spoke of something else. You can remember, looking back, no special expression on anyone's face?' Poirot continued his questioning.

'No.'

'And the very next day, *Cora is killed* – and you ask yourself, "Was she killed because what she had said was true?" Me, I think, <u>*mon cher*</u>, exactly as you thought – that there is a case for investigation. You have spoken of these matters to the police?'

'No. I represent the family, Poirot. And if Richard Abernethie *was* murdered, there seems only one way it could have been done.'

'By poison?'

'Exactly. *And the body has been cremated.* There is now no <u>evidence</u> available. But I, myself, *must* be sure about it. That is why, Poirot, I have come to *you*.'

'Who was in the house at the time of his death?'

'Lanscombe – an old butler who has been with him for years, a cook and a housemaid. If he was murdered, one of them must be the killer.'

'Ah no! This Cora, she knows Richard Abernethie was killed, yet she agrees to keeping it quiet. Therefore it *must* be one of the family who is responsible. But we shall never be able to prove anything in the case of Richard Abernethie. However, the murder of Cora Lansquenet is different. Once we know "who" then it should be possible to get the evidence we need. You have already done something?' Poirot asked.

'I hoped that by a few casual questions I could clear certain members of the family from suspicion, perhaps *all* of them. In which case, Cora would have been wrong and her own death must have been done by a criminal who broke in. After all, it is simple. What were the members of the Abernethie family doing on the afternoon that Cora Lansquenet was killed?'

'*Eh bien*,' said Poirot, 'what *were* they doing?'

'George Crossfield was at Hurst Park horse-races. Rosamund Shane was shopping in London. Her husband was at lunch discussing a play. Susan and Gregory Banks were at home all day. Timothy Abernethie was at his home in Yorkshire, and his wife was driving herself home from Enderby.'

Hercule Poirot nodded. 'Yes, that is what they *say*. And is it all true?'

'I don't know, Poirot. George *may* have been at Hurst Park races, but I do not think he was. He said that he had bet on a couple of winners. I asked him the names and both horses he named had, I found, been expected to win – but only one had.'

'Interesting. Had this George any urgent need for money at the time of his uncle's death?'

'I have no evidence, but I suspect that he has been <u>gambling</u> with his clients' money.' He sighed. 'As for Rosamund, she is lovely, but not very intelligent. Her husband, Michael Shane, is a man with <u>ambition</u>. But I have no reason to suspect him of a violent crime. However, until I know that he really was doing what he says he was doing, I cannot take him off my list of <u>suspects</u>.'

'You have no doubts about Rosamund, the wife?'

'No – no – she is a delicate-looking creature.'

'And beautiful!' said Poirot with a smile. 'And the other niece?'

'Susan? She is a girl of huge ability, I think. She and her husband were at home together that day. I said that I had tried to telephone them on the afternoon in question – I hadn't, of course. Greg said very quickly that the telephone had not been working all day.'

'So again there is no evidence . . . What is the husband like?'

'He does not have a pleasing personality, though I cannot say exactly why. Susan has the mental strength and intelligence of Richard Abernethie. But I feel that she lacks the kindness and warmth of my old friend.'

'Women are never kind,' remarked Poirot. 'Though they can sometimes be gentle. Does she love her husband?'

'She loves him almost too much, I would say.'

'Me, I am not so sentimental about beautiful young ladies! Now tell me about your visit to the older members of the Abernethie family.'

Mr Entwhistle described his visit to Timothy and Maude and Poirot nodded.

'So Mrs Maude Abernethie is a good car mechanic. And Mr Timothy Abernethie is not the sick man he likes to think himself. He also resented his brother's success. What about the sixth beneficiary?'

'Helen? I do not suspect her for a moment. Anyway, she was at Enderby. With three servants in the house.'

'Eh bien, my friend,' said Poirot. 'What do you want me to do?'

'I want to know the truth, Poirot. I know you don't take cases any more, but I ask you to take this one. And I will be responsible for your fees. Come now, money is always useful.'

Poirot smiled. 'Not if it all goes in the taxes! But I will admit, your problem interests me! Because it is not easy . . . But I think it will be best if you yourself talk to the doctor who was looking after Mr Richard Abernethie. He will speak more freely to you than to me. Ask him about Mr Abernethie's illness. Find out what medicines Mr Abernethie was taking at the time of his death and even before. Find out if he ever said anything to his doctor about being poisoned. By the way, this Miss Gilchrist is sure that he used the term *poisoned* in talking to his sister?'

Mr Entwhistle thought for a moment. 'It was the word she used – but she is the sort of <u>witness</u> who might change the actual words used, thinking that complete accuracy isn't important. I can talk to her again.'

'Yes. Or I will do so.' Poirot now said in a different voice, 'Has it occurred to you that your Miss Gilchrist may be in some danger herself? Cora spoke her suspicions on the day of the funeral. The question in the murderer's mind will be, did Cora tell them to anybody when she first heard of Richard's death? And the most likely person for her to have spoken to about them would be Miss Gilchrist. I think, *mon cher*, that she should not be alone in that cottage!'

Chapter 8

Dr Larraby, when questioned by Mr Entwhistle about the possibility of Richard Abernethie being poisoned, <u>denied</u> it at once. 'Entwhistle, *who* is making this suggestion?'

'Abernethie never even suggested that one of his relations wanted him out of the way?' Mr Entwhistle asked.

'No!'

Mr Entwhistle told him of Cora's comment at the funeral and Dr Larraby smiled.

'My dear <u>fellow</u>, the explanation for that is simple. The woman is at a certain time of life – searching for excitement, unbalanced, unreliable. She might say anything. They do, you know!'

'You may be right,' Mr Entwhistle said, standing up. 'Unfortunately we can't ask her as she's been murdered herself.'

'What?'

'You've probably read about it in the paper. Mrs Lansquenet at Lytchett St Mary in Berkshire.'

'I had no idea she was a relation of Richard Abernethie's!' Dr Larraby was looking worried now.

★ ★ ★

Back at Enderby, Mr Entwhistle asked the old butler what his plans were.

'Mrs Helen Abernethie has asked me to stay on until the house is sold, Sir.' He sighed. 'I appreciate Mr Richard's <u>generosity</u> to me in his will, and though my married niece has asked me to go and live with them, well, it won't be the same as living at Enderby.'

'I know,' said Mr Entwhistle. 'It's a hard new world for us old men. I wish I had seen more of my old friend before he died. How did he seem those last few months?'

'Well, he wasn't himself, Sir, not since Mr Mortimer's death.'

'No. And he was a sick man – sick men have strange ideas sometimes. I imagine Mr Abernethie did, too. Did he speak of enemies sometimes, of somebody wishing to hurt him – perhaps? He might even have thought his food was being poisoned?'

Old Lanscombe looked surprised. 'I don't remember anything of that kind, Sir.'

'He invited some of his family to stay with him, didn't he, before he died? His nephew and his two nieces and their husbands? Was he satisfied with those visits? Or was he disappointed?'

Lanscombe's eyes became cold. 'I really could not say, Sir.'

'I think you could,' said Mr Entwhistle gently. 'I liked your Master very much and so did you. That's why I'm asking you for your opinion as a *man*, not as a butler. Did you feel that something was – wrong?'

'Only since the funeral, Sir. And I couldn't say exactly what it is.'

'You know the contents of the will?'

'Yes, Sir. Mrs Helen thought I would like to know. It seemed to me a very fair will.'

'Yes, but it is not, I think, the will that Mr Abernethie originally intended to make after his son died.'

'The Master, Sir, was very disappointed after Mr George had been here . . . Miss Susan he liked at once, but he didn't like her husband at all.'

'And the other couple?'

'I think the Master enjoyed having them here – but he never approved of acting as a job. He said to me one day, "It's a silly kind of life. It seems to me that actors and actresses live in a world of make-believe. I'm not sure it helps their judgment of what is right and what is wrong." Of course he wasn't speaking directly.'

'No, no, I understand. Now after these visits, Mr Abernethie himself went away – first to his brother, and afterwards to Mrs Lansquenet. Can you remember anything he said about those visits on his return?'

'The Master used to talk quietly to himself sometimes – thinking aloud – when I was in the room. He said something about not understanding what had happened to the money their father had left Timothy. And then he said something like, "Women can be fools in ninety-nine different ways but not in the hundredth." And "You can only say what you really think to someone of your own generation. They don't think you're imagining things as the younger ones do." And later he said "It's not very pleasant to have to set traps for people, but I don't see what else I can do."'

Richard Abernethie had spoken of setting a trap. For whom?

* * *

Mr Entwhistle decided he should take Helen into his confidence. 'I am going to ask you if you could stay here until the house is sold,' he said, 'but there is another reason why I would be grateful if you would stay on. There is a friend of mine, a man called Hercule Poirot –'

Helen said sharply, 'Hercule Poirot?'

'You know of him?'

'Yes.' Her face was white. 'You think – that Cora was right? That Richard was – *murdered*?'

Mr Entwhistle told her everything. When he had finished she said, 'Maude and I, that night after the funeral – it was in both our minds, I'm sure. And then – Cora was killed – and I told myself it was just coincidence – but oh! If I could only be sure.

I've been uneasy . . . Not just about what Cora said that day – something else. Something that I felt at the time to be wrong.'

'Wrong? In what way?'

'That's just it. I don't know.'

'You mean it was something about one of the people in the room?'

'Yes – yes – something of that kind. But I can't remember what it *was*. The more I think . . .'

'Don't think. That is the wrong way to try to remember something. Let it go. Sooner or later it will come into your mind. And when it does – let me know – at once.'

'I will.'

Chapter 9

The front-door bell rang and for some reason Miss Gilchrist felt nervous. She went <u>unwillingly</u> to the door, telling herself not to be so silly.

A young woman dressed in black and carrying a small suitcase was standing on the step outside. She noticed the nervous look on Miss Gilchrist's face and said quickly, 'Miss Gilchrist? I am Mrs Lansquenet's niece – Susan Banks.'

'Oh dear, yes, of course. Do come in, Mrs Banks. I didn't know you were coming down for the inquest. I would have had something ready – coffee or tea.'

Susan Banks said quickly, 'I don't want anything. I'm so sorry if I frightened you.'

'Well, I'm not usually nervous, but – perhaps it's just the inquest – I have been nervous all this morning. Half an hour ago the bell rang and I was almost too afraid to open the door – which was really very stupid as it is so unlikely that a murderer would come *back* – and it was only a <u>nun</u>, collecting for an <u>orphanage</u>. Did you come here by train?'

'No, I came by car. I thought the road was too narrow to park outside so I drove the car on a little way past the cottage and found an old <u>quarry</u> and parked there.'

Susan Banks looked round the sitting room with interest. 'Poor Aunt Cora. She left what she had to me, you know.'

'Yes, I know. I expect you'll need the furniture. You're newly married, I understand.'

'I don't want any of it,' Susan said. 'I will sell it. Unless – is there any of it you would like? I'd be very happy . . .' She stopped, a little embarrassed. But Miss Gilchrist gave a big smile. 'Now that's *very* kind of you, Mrs Banks – but I <u>put my own</u>

<u>things in store</u> in case — some day — I would need them. I had a small tearoom at one time, you know — then the war came . . . But I didn't sell everything, because I did hope to have my own little home again one day, so I put the best things in store with my father's pictures. But I *would* like very much, if you *really* wouldn't mind, to have that little painted tea table. Such a pretty thing and we always had tea on it.'

Susan, looking at what *she* thought was an ugly green table painted with large purple flowers, said that she would be delighted for Miss Gilchrist to have it.

'Thank you *very* much, Mrs Banks. I imagine you would like to look through her things? After the inquest, perhaps?' Miss Gilchrist asked.

'I thought I'd stay here a couple of days and clear everything up.'

'Sleep here, you mean?'

'Yes. Is there any difficulty?'

'Oh no, I'll put fresh sheets on my bed, and I can sleep down here on the couch.'

'But there's Aunt Cora's room, isn't there? I can sleep in that.'

'You — you wouldn't mind?'

'You mean because she was murdered there? Oh no. I'm very practical, Miss Gilchrist. It's been — I mean — it's been cleaned?'

'Oh *yes*, Mrs Banks. All the blankets were sent away to the laundry and the whole room was cleaned thoroughly.'

She led the way upstairs. The room where Cora Lansquenet had died was clean and fresh and had no <u>sinister</u> atmosphere. Over the fireplace an oil painting showed a young woman about to enter her bath.

Susan gave a slight <u>shudder</u> as she looked at it and Miss Gilchrist said, 'That was painted by Mrs Lansquenet's husband. There are a lot more of his pictures in the dining room.'

'How terrible! Where are Aunt Cora's own pictures?'

'In my room. Would you like to see them?'

Miss Gilchrist proudly showed her the paintings.

Susan commented that it looked like Aunt Cora was very fond of villages by the sea and that perhaps her paintings, which were very detailed and very brightly coloured, might have been painted from picture postcards.

But Miss Gilchrist was <u>indignant</u>. Mrs Lansquenet *always* painted from nature!

'Mrs Lansquenet was a real artist,' said Miss Gilchrist sharply. She looked at her watch and Susan said quickly, 'Yes, we ought to leave for the inquest. Is it far? Shall I get the car?'

It was only five minutes' walk, Miss Gilchrist said, so they left together on foot. Mr Entwhistle, who had travelled by train, met them at the Village Hall.

At the inquest, the dead woman was identified. It was said that death was unlikely to have occurred later than four-thirty. Miss Gilchrist <u>testified</u> to finding the body. A police constable and Inspector Morton gave their evidence and the <u>jury</u> was quick to reach the <u>verdict</u>: *Murder by some person or persons unknown.*

Afterwards, when they came out again into the sunlight, half a dozen newspaper cameras clicked. Mr Entwhistle took them into the *King's Arms* <u>pub</u> for lunch in a private room. He said to Susan, 'I had no idea you were coming down today, Susan. We could have come together. Did your husband come with you?'

'Greg had some important things to do. We've got great plans for the future – we are going to open a beauty salon, which I will run, and a laboratory where Greg can make face creams.'

Mr Entwhistle's mind went to other things. When Susan had spoken to him twice without his answering, he apologized.

'Forgive me, my dear, I was thinking about your Uncle Timothy. I am a little worried.'

'I wouldn't worry. Uncle Timothy is not ill at all – he's just a hypochondriac.'

'It is not *his* health that is worrying me. It's Maude's. Apparently she has fallen downstairs and broken her ankle. She's got to stay in bed and your uncle is terribly worried.'

'Because he'll have to look after her instead of the other way around? It will do him a lot of good,' said Susan.

'Yes – yes, but will your poor aunt *get* any looking after?'

They came out of the *King's Arms*, rather warily but the newspaper reporters and photographers had gone.

Mr Entwhistle took them back to the cottage then returned to the *King's Arms* where he had booked a room. The funeral was to be on the following day.

'My car's still in the quarry,' said Susan when she and Miss Gilchrist had gone inside. 'I'll go and get it and drive it along to the village later.'

Miss Gilchrist said anxiously, 'You will do that in daylight, won't you?'

Susan laughed. 'You don't think the murderer is still nearby, do you?'

'No – no, I suppose not.' Miss Gilchrist looked embarrassed.

But it's exactly what she does think, thought Susan.

Miss Gilchrist went towards the kitchen. 'I'm sure you'd like tea, Mrs Banks!'

Susan went into the sitting room. She had only been there a few minutes when the doorbell rang. Susan went to the front door and opened it. An elderly gentleman said, smiling, 'My name is Alexander Guthrie. I was a very old friend of Cora Lansquenet's. May I ask who you are?'

'I am Susan Abernethie – well, Banks now since I married. Cora was my aunt. Please come in.'

'Thank you.' Mr Guthrie followed Susan into the sitting room.

'This is a sad occasion,' said Mr Guthrie. 'Yes, a very sad occasion. I felt the least I could do was to attend the inquest – and of course the funeral. I usually visited Cora once a year, and recently she had been buying pictures at local sales, and wanted me to look at some of them. I am an art critic, you know. Of course most of the paintings Cora bought were terrible; last year she wanted me to come and look at a Rembrandt she had bought. A Rembrandt! It wasn't even a good copy of one!'

'Like that one over there, I expect,' said Susan, pointing to the wall behind him.

Mr Guthrie got up and went over to study the picture. 'Poor dear Cora. Dirt,' he said, 'is a wonderful thing, Mrs Banks! It gives a sort of romance to the most terrible paintings.'

'There are some more pictures in the dining room,' said Susan, 'but I think they are all her husband's work.'

Mr Guthrie held up a hand. 'Do not make me look at those again. I always tried not to hurt Cora's feelings. A loving wife – a very loving wife. Well, dear Mrs Banks, I must not take up more of your time.'

'Oh, do stay and have some tea. I think it's nearly ready.'

'That is very kind of you.' Mr Guthrie sat down again.

'I'll just go and see.'

In the kitchen, Miss Gilchrist was lifting a tray from the oven.

'There's a Mr Guthrie here,' Susan said. 'I've asked him to stay for tea.'

'Mr Guthrie? Oh, yes, he was a great friend of dear Mrs Lansquenet's. How lucky; I've made scones and there's some homemade strawberry jam.'

Susan took in the tray and Miss Gilchrist, following with teapot and kettle, greeted Mr Guthrie.

'Hot scones, how lovely,' said Mr Guthrie.

Miss Gilchrist was delighted. The scones were excellent. The memory of the Willow Tree tearoom seemed to be in the room with them. Miss Gilchrist was clearly doing what she had been born to do.

'I do feel rather guilty,' said Mr Guthrie, 'enjoying my tea here, where poor Cora was so horribly murdered.'

Miss Gilchrist shook her head. 'No, no. Mrs Lansquenet would have wanted you to have a good tea.'

'Perhaps you are right. The fact is that it's difficult for me to accept that someone I knew – actually knew – has been murdered! And certainly not by some casual thief who broke in and attacked her. I *can* imagine, you know, reasons why *Cora* might have been murdered –'

Susan said quickly, 'Can you? What reasons?'

'Well, if she knew a secret, she would always want to talk about it. Even if she promised not to, she would still do it. She couldn't stop herself. So a little poison in a cup of tea – *that* would not have surprised me. And I would have thought she had very little to take that would be worth it for a burglar. Ah! Well, there's a lot of crime about since the war. Times have changed.'

Thanking them for the tea, he said goodbye. Miss Gilchrist took him to the door and came back into the room with a small parcel in her hand. 'The postman must have been while we were at the inquest. He must have pushed this through the letterbox and it fell in the corner behind the door.'

Happily Miss Gilchrist tore off the paper. Inside was a small white box tied with silver ribbon. 'It's wedding cake!' She pulled off the ribbon. Inside was a slice of rich fruitcake with white icing. 'How nice! Now who –' She read the card attached. '*John and Mary*. Now who *can* that be? How silly to put no surname. It might be my old friend Dorothy's daughter – but I haven't heard of an engagement or a marriage. Then there's the Enfield girl – no, her name was Margaret. No address or anything. Oh well, I suppose I'll remember soon . . .'

Chapter 10

Susan drove her car to the *King's Arms'* car park where she left it by a <u>chauffeur-driven</u> <u>Daimler</u> which was preparing to go out. Inside it was an elderly foreign gentleman with a large moustache.

After supper, Susan questioned Miss Gilchrist about her uncle's visit to Cora.

'Did they get on well together?'

'Oh, yes. She did say that he had got very old – I think she said senile . . .'

'But *you* didn't think he was senile?'

'Well, not to *look* at. But I didn't talk to him much, I left them alone together.'

Was Miss Gilchrist the kind of woman who listened at doors? She was honest, Susan felt sure, but . . .

'You didn't hear any of their conversation?' Susan asked. 'Sometimes, in these small cottages, you can't avoid overhearing, and now that they are dead, it's really important to the family to know what was said at that meeting.'

Miss Gilchrist nodded. 'I think they were talking about Mr Abernethie's health – and certain – well, ideas, he had. He blamed his ill-health on *other people*. A common thing, I believe, in the old. My aunt . . .'

'Yes,' Susan interrupted, 'my uncle's servants were upset by his thinking . . . It *was* the servants he suspected, I suppose? Of poisoning him, I mean?'

'I don't know. I – really don't know.' But she looked away from Susan, so perhaps Miss Gilchrist knew more than she was willing to admit.

42

Susan decided not to say any more on the subject until later and asked instead, 'What are your own plans for the future?'

'Well, I told Mr Entwhistle I would be happy to stay on until everything here was cleared up and I wanted to ask you how long that was likely to be, because, of course, I must start looking about for another job as a companion.'

Susan thought for a moment. 'There's really not very much to be done here, but I wanted to tell you – that I hope you'll accept three months' salary.'

'That's very generous of you, Mrs Banks. I do appreciate it. And you would say that I had been with a relation of yours and that I had – proved satisfactory?'

'Oh, of course.'

'I don't know whether I ought to ask it.' Miss Gilchrist's hands began to shake and she tried to steady her voice. 'But would it be possible not to – to mention what happened here – or even the *name*?'

Susan stared. 'I don't understand.'

'Because it's *murder*. A murder that's been in the papers and that everybody has read about. People might think, "Two women living together, and one of them is killed – *perhaps the companion did it*." It's been worrying me terribly, Mrs Banks, thinking that perhaps I'll never get another job – not of this kind. And what else is there that I can do?'

Susan suddenly realized the <u>desperation</u> of this woman who was <u>dependent on</u> other peoples' good opinion to get a job. It was true that Miss Gilchrist did not benefit from Cora Lansquenet's death – but who would know that?

Susan spoke with her usual confidence. 'Don't worry,' she said, as Miss Gilchrist got up to take their coffee cups into the kitchen, 'I'm sure I can find you a job amongst my friends. There won't be any difficulty.'

And just moments later an idea came to her. Of course, Susan said to herself. That would be perfect! And she went to the telephone . . .

Soon afterwards Susan went into the kitchen. 'I've just been talking to my Uncle Timothy. Would you like to go to Yorkshire and look after my aunt? She fell and broke her ankle, as you know. You could cook and look after Aunt Maude.'

Miss Gilchrist almost dropped the coffee pot in her excitement. 'Oh, thank you, thank you – that really is kind. I am really good at looking after sick people, and I'm sure I can manage your uncle and cook him nice little meals. It's really very kind of you, Mrs Banks, and I *do* appreciate it.'

Chapter 11

Susan lay in bed, her mind racing. She had said she did not mind sleeping in this bed where Aunt Cora . . .

No, no she must not think about that. Think ahead – her future and Greg's. The building in Cardigan Street – it was just what they wanted. They could have the beauty salon on the ground floor and live in the lovely flat upstairs. And there was a room out at the back for a laboratory for Greg. And Greg would get calm and well again. There would be no more of those huge angers; of those times when he looked at her without seeming to know who she was. Once or twice she'd been really frightened. And it would have happened again if Uncle Richard hadn't died just when he did.

Uncle Richard had nothing to live for, so his death was a good thing, really. If only she could sleep. She always felt so safe in town – surrounded by people – never alone. Whereas here . . . Why did she feel that there was someone in this room, someone close beside her?

Surely that was a <u>groan</u>? Someone in pain – someone dying! I mustn't imagine things, I mustn't, I mustn't, Susan whispered to herself. There it was again . . . someone groaning in great pain. This was real! The groans came from the room next door.

Susan jumped out of bed and went into Miss Gilchrist's room. She was sitting up in bed, her face twisted with pain. She tried to get out of bed but was very sick and then collapsed back on the pillows.

'Please – ring the doctor. I – I must have eaten something . . .'

★ ★ ★

As soon as the doctor examined Miss Gilchrist, he sent for an ambulance.

'She's really bad then?' asked Susan.

'Yes. I've given her <u>morphia</u> to ease the pain. But it looks . . .' He paused. 'What has she eaten?'

'We had macaroni and cheese for dinner and a milk pudding and then coffee afterwards.'

'Did you have the same things?'

'Yes.'

'And she's eaten nothing else? No tinned fish? Or sausages?'

'No.'

The ambulance came and took Miss Gilchrist away. The doctor went with her. When he had left, Susan went upstairs to bed. This time she fell asleep as soon as her head touched the pillow.

★ ★ ★

A large number of people came to Cora Lansquenet's funeral. Most of the villagers were there and wreaths had been sent by the other members of the family. Mr Entwhistle asked where Miss Gilchrist was, and Susan explained. Mr Entwhistle was surprised. 'Wasn't that strange?'

'Oh, she's better this morning. They called from the hospital. People do get these stomach upsets.'

Mr Entwhistle said no more. He was returning to London immediately after the funeral.

Susan went back to the cottage and made herself an omelette. Then she went up to Cora's room and started to sort through the dead woman's things.

She was interrupted by the arrival of the doctor, who was looking worried.

'Mrs Banks, will you tell me again exactly what Miss Gilchrist had to eat and drink yesterday. Everything. There must have been something she had and you didn't?'

'I don't think so . . . scones, jam, tea – and then supper. No, I can't remember anything. Was it food poisoning?'

'It was <u>arsenic</u>,' he said.

'Arsenic? You mean somebody gave her arsenic?'

'That's what it looks like.'

'Could the arsenic have got into her food or drink by accident?'

'It seems very unlikely, although such things have been known. But if you and she ate the same things . . .'

Susan gave a sudden exclamation. 'Why, of course, the wedding cake! I didn't have any of that, though she offered me some.' Susan explained about the cake that had arrived.

'Strange. And you say she wasn't sure who sent it? Is there any of it left? Or is the box it came in still here somewhere?'

'I don't know.'

They found the white box in the kitchen with a few very small pieces of cake still in it.

'I'll take this,' the doctor said. 'Do you have any idea where the wrapping paper it came in might be?' They looked but they did not find it.

'You won't be leaving here just yet, Mrs Banks?' His voice was friendly, but it made Susan feel a little uncomfortable. 'No, I will be here for a few days.'

'Good. You understand the police will probably want to ask some questions. You don't know of anyone who – well, might have wanted to hurt Miss Gilchrist?'

Susan shook her head. 'I don't really know much about her. She was with my aunt for some years – that's all I know.'

'Right. Well, I must go now.'

The cottage felt hot and uncomfortable and when he had gone Susan left the front door wide open and she went slowly upstairs to continue going through Aunt Cora's belongings.

There was a box full of old photographs and drawing books. Susan put them to one side, sorted all the papers she had found, and began to go through them. About a quarter way through she came to a letter. She read it twice and was still staring at it, when a voice behind her made her give a cry of fear.

'And what have you got hold of there, Susan? Hello, what's the matter?'

'George? How you frightened me!'

Her cousin smiled at her. 'So it seems.'

'How did you get here?'

'Well, the front door was open, so I walked in. There was nobody about on the ground floor, so I came up here. If you mean how did I get to this part of the world, I decided this morning to come to the funeral, but the car broke down, then seemed to start working again. I was too late for the funeral by then, but I thought I might as well continue the journey because I rang your flat and Greg told me you'd come to sort things out. I thought I might help you.'

Susan said, 'Can you take days off whenever you like?'

'A funeral has always been an acceptable excuse for taking a day off. Anyway, I won't be going to the office in future – not now that I'm rich. I will have better things to do.' He paused and smiled, 'Same as Greg.'

Susan had never seen much of this cousin of hers and had always found him rather difficult to understand. 'Why did you really come down here, George?'

'I came to do a little detective work to try and find out whether Aunt Cora really did know that someone had killed Uncle Richard. Now, what's in that letter that you were reading so carefully when I came in?'

'It's a letter that Uncle Richard wrote to Cora after he'd been here to see her.'

How very black George's eyes were; and black eyes hid the thoughts that lay behind them.

George said slowly, 'Anything interesting in it?'

'No, not exactly . . .'

'Can I see?'

She hesitated for a moment, then put the letter into his hand.

He read some of it aloud. '*Pleased to have seen you again after all these years . . . looking very well . . . had a good journey home and arrived back not too tired . . .*' His voice changed suddenly, '*Please don't say anything to anyone about what I told you. It may be a mistake. Your loving brother, Richard.*'

He looked up at Susan. 'What does that mean?'

'It might mean anything . . .'

'Oh yes, but it does suggest something. Does anyone know what he told Cora?'

'Miss Gilchrist might know,' said Susan. 'I think she listened at the door to them. But she's in hospital; she's got arsenic poisoning.'

'You don't mean it?' George exclaimed.

'I do. Someone sent her some poisoned wedding cake.'

George whistled. 'It looks,' he said, 'as though Uncle Richard was not mistaken when he talked about being poisoned himself.'

★ ★ ★

The following morning Inspector Morton called at the cottage. 'Arsenic was found in the small pieces of wedding cake that Dr Proctor took from here. Miss Gilchrist keeps saying that nobody would do such a thing. But somebody did. You don't know anything that might help us, Mrs Banks?'

Susan shook her head.

'Well, young Andrews, the driver of the post van, doesn't remember delivering the parcel with the wedding cake in it. He can't be sure, though, so there's a doubt about it.'

'But – what's the alternative?'

'The alternative, Mrs Banks, is that an old piece of brown paper was used to wrap the parcel that already had Miss Gilchrist's name and address on it and a used postage stamp. That package was then pushed through the letter box or put inside the door by hand to make her think that it had come by post. It's a clever idea to choose wedding cake. Lonely middle-aged women are sentimental about wedding cake because they are so pleased to have been remembered by the young couple.'

'Was there enough poison in it to – kill?'

'That depends on whether Miss Gilchrist ate all of it. She thinks that she didn't, so I'd like to go upstairs if you don't mind, Mrs Banks.'

'Of course.' She followed him up to Miss Gilchrist's room and said, 'I'm afraid it's in a terrible state. I didn't have time to clean up before the funeral and then after Dr Proctor came I thought perhaps I ought to leave it as it was.'

'That was very intelligent of you, Mrs Banks.' He went to the bed and lifted the pillow. 'There you are,' he said, smiling.

A piece of wedding cake lay on the sheet.

'How extraordinary,' said Susan.

'Oh no, it's not. Perhaps your generation doesn't do it. But it's an old <u>custom</u>. They say that if you put a piece of wedding cake under your pillow, you'll dream of your future husband. Miss Gilchrist didn't want to tell us about it, I suspect, because she felt silly doing such a thing at her age. But I thought that's what it might be.' His face became serious. 'And if it hadn't been for an <u>old maid's</u> foolishness, Miss Gilchrist might not be alive today.'

Chapter 12

Two elderly men sat together in a room where everything was square. Almost the only exception was Hercule Poirot: whose stomach was pleasantly rounded, his head looked like an egg in shape, and his moustache curved upwards flamboyantly.

He was looking thoughtfully at Mr Goby, who was small and thin. Mr Goby was famous for collecting information. Very few people knew about him and very few employed his services – but those few were usually extremely rich. They had to be, for Mr Goby was very expensive. His speciality was getting information – quickly. At a word from Mr Goby, hundreds of men and women, old and young, who worked for him, went out to question, investigate, and get results. Mr Goby had now almost retired from business. But he occasionally worked for a few old clients. Hercule Poirot was one of these.

Mr Goby was not looking at Hercule Poirot because Mr Goby never looked directly at anybody. Right now he seemed to be talking to the fireplace. 'I've got what information I could for you. Nowadays you can walk in almost anywhere with a notebook and pencil and ask people all about their lives and they won't doubt for a minute that you are working for the Government – and that the Government really wants to know! Yes, Government snooping is a gift to investigators and long may it continue!

'Now,' said Mr Goby, and took out a little notebook and turned over the pages. 'Here we are. Mr George Crossfield. He's been in debt for a while now. He's been using money from his clients' trust funds. For three months he's been worried and bad-tempered in the office. But since his uncle's death that's all changed!

'What he said about being at Hurst Park races is almost certainly untrue. None of the people he usually places his bets with saw him. Nobody saw him in Lytchett St Mary either, but that doesn't mean he wasn't there. There are other ways to approach the cottage than through the village. He acted in plays at university, by the way. So if he went to the cottage that day, he could have used make up to change the way he looks. I'll keep him in my book, shall I?'

'You may keep him in,' said Hercule Poirot.

Mr Goby turned another page. 'Mr Michael Shane. He likes money and is very attractive to women. He's been having an affair with Sorrel Dainton, the actress, and his wife Rosamund doesn't know about it. She doesn't know much about anything, it seems. She's not a good actress, and is crazy about her husband.

'On the day Mr Shane says he was meeting a Mr Rosenheim and a Mr Oscar Lewis for lunch to discuss a play, he sent them a telegram to say he couldn't come. What he *did* do was to go to the Emeraldo Car people and hire a car at about twelve o'clock. He returned it at about six in the evening. The car had been driven just about the right number of miles, but it was not seen in Lytchett St Mary that day. However, there are lots of places he could have left it hidden a mile or so away; there's even an old quarry a few hundred yards down the road from the cottage. Do we keep Mr Shane in?'

'Most certainly.'

'Now *Mrs* Shane.' Mr Goby told his left sleeve about Rosamund Shane. 'She says she was shopping. And she had heard she had inherited money the day before. She has accounts in a number of shops but she hasn't paid her bills, so it's possible that she went in here and there, trying on clothes, looking at jewellery, checking prices – and not buying anything! I asked one of my young ladies, who's knowledgeable about the theatre and the people in it, to follow her and stop by her table in a restaurant, She exclaimed the way they do, "Darling, I haven't seen you since *Way Down Under*. You were *wonderful* in that!" In a minute they were talking theatrical stuff and my girl then said, "I believe I saw you at so and so, on so and so," giving the day. Most ladies are tricked by that and say, "Oh no, I was . . ." whatever it may be. But Mrs Shane just looked blank and said, "Oh, maybe. I couldn't possibly remember." What can you do with a lady like that?' Mr Goby shook his head sadly.

'Nothing,' said Hercule Poirot with some feeling. 'I shall never forget the killing of Lord Edgware. I was nearly <u>defeated</u> – yes, I, Hercule Poirot – by the extremely simple cleverness of an empty brain. Very simple-minded people often have the unexpected intelligence to commit a simple crime and then leave it alone. Let us hope that our murderer is intelligent and thoroughly pleased with himself and unable to resist <u>showing off</u>. But continue.'

Once more Mr Goby looked at his little book. 'Mr and Mrs Banks said they were at home all day. Well, Susan Banks wasn't. She went round to the garage, got out her car, and drove off in it at about one o'clock. We do not know where she went and she came back at about five. I have no idea how many miles she did that day because she drives every day and, unlike Michael Shane's hired car, no one keeps a note of the mileage.

'As for Mr Gregory Banks, we don't know *what* he did. He didn't go to work and it seems he had already asked for a couple of days off because of the funeral. Since then he's left his job – where they do not like Mr Banks. He used to become very angry at even small things that upset him. Until about four months ago – just before he met his wife and joined this particular chemist's shop – he was in a <u>nursing home</u> as a patient. He had made some mistake with a medicine he made for a customer at the pharmacy he worked at then. The woman recovered, and there was no <u>prosecution</u>. The shop didn't <u>sack</u> him, but he <u>resigned</u> and told the doctor he was filled with guilt – that he had done it deliberately. He said that the woman had been rude to him when she came into the shop, and so he had added an almost <u>lethal dose</u> of some drug or other to her medicine. "She had to be punished for speaking to me like that!" was what he said. The doctors don't believe it was deliberate at all, he was just careless, but they say that he wanted to make it important and serious. Anyway, this nursing home cured him and sent him home, and he met Susan Abernethie. He got the job he's just left and another pharmacist at the same shop said he had a very bad temper.'

'Mon ami,' said Hercule Poirot. 'It really amazes me how you get your information! Medical and highly <u>confidential</u> most of it!'

Mr Goby said, looking at the door, that there were *ways* . . . 'Now we come to Mr and Mrs Timothy Abernethie. They are very short of money. Mr Abernethie enjoys being ill and the emphasis is on the enjoyment. He has everyone fetching and carrying things for him because he says he's too ill to do anything for himself, but he eats large meals, and seems strong physically. There's no one in the house after the daily cleaning woman leaves, and she says he was in a very bad temper on the morning of the day after the funeral. He was alone in the house and nobody saw him from 9.30 that morning until the following morning.'

'And Mrs Maude Abernethie?'

'Everyone says she is a very nice lady. She left Enderby by car and arrived on foot at a small garage in a village on the way. She explained that her car had broken down a couple of miles away.

'A mechanic drove her out to it and said they would have to get it in to the garage and it would be a long job. The lady went to a small hotel, arranged to stay the night, and asked for some sandwiches to take with her as she said she would like to go out walking and see something of the countryside. She didn't come back to the hotel till late that evening.'

'And the times?'

'She got the sandwiches at eleven. If she had walked to the main road, a mile away, she could have got a lift into a town called Wallcaster and caught an express train which stops near Lytchett St Mary. It *could* just have been done if the murder had happened fairly late in the afternoon.'

'What exactly *was* wrong with the car?'

'Do you want the exact details, Monsieur Poirot?'

'No, no! I have no mechanical knowledge.'

'It was a difficult thing to find. And also to fix. And it *could* have been done deliberately by someone who was familiar with the insides of a car.'

'Wonderful!' said Poirot. 'Can we clear *nobody* from suspicion? And Mrs Helen Abernethie?'

'She's a very nice lady, too, and Mr Richard Abernethie was very fond of her. She came there to stay about two weeks before he died.'

'Was that after he had been to Lytchett St Mary to see his sister?'

'No, just before. Mrs Helen's income is less, since the war, than it used to be. She has a house in Cyprus and spends part of the year there. She also has a young nephew whose school fees she is paying.'

Poirot shut his eyes. 'And it was impossible for her to have left Enderby that day without the servants knowing? Say that is so, I beg you!'

Mr Goby looked down at Poirot's shoes. 'I'm afraid I can't say that, Monsieur Poirot. Mrs Abernethie went to London to get some extra clothes because she had agreed with Mr Entwhistle to stay on and see to things.'

Chapter 13

Inspector Morton came straight to the point. 'I had to come to London,' he said. 'And I found your address, Monsieur Poirot. I was interested to see you at the inquest on Thursday and I came to ask if you could help us at all. *Something* must have brought you down there, Monsieur Poirot, and there have been developments.' And he told him about the poisoned wedding cake.

Poirot took a deep, slow breath. 'I warned Mr Entwhistle to look after Miss Gilchrist. An attack on her was always a possibility. But I must admit that I did *not* expect poison.'

'But *why* did you think she might be attacked?'

Poirot said, 'It begins, all this, at a funeral. Or rather, to be exact, *after* the funeral.' And he told the story as Mr Entwhistle had told it to him. Then Poirot continued, 'This attempt to silence Miss Gilchrist, it is a mistake. For now there are *two* events which you need to investigate further.'

'Yes. Well, if the postman *did* deliver the wedding cake, it seems odd that the parcel wasn't noticed until after this Mr Guthrie came. We're checking up on him, of course. *He* could have placed that parcel where Miss Gilchrist found it. Now, Mr George Crossfield was in the area next day. What do you know about him, Monsieur Poirot?'

'Not as much as I would like to.'

'It's like that, is it? There are quite a lot of people who are interested in the late Mr Abernethie's will, I understand. I hope it doesn't mean investigating all of them!'

'I have a little information which you may not have. Naturally *I* have no authority to ask these people questions. In fact, it would not be wise for me to do so.'

'I will go slowly myself,' said Morton. 'I don't want to warn anyone until it suits me to.'

Poirot smiled. 'A very wise way of working. For myself, I go to Enderby Hall. It is *people* that I am interested in. I will pretend to buy, I believe, a big country house for foreign <u>refugees</u>. I will represent U.N.A.R.C.O.'

'And what's U.N.A.R.C.O.?' asked Morton, puzzled.

'The United Nations Aid for Refugee Centre Organization. It sounds appropriate, do you not think? And Enderby Hall might be just right. I will, of course tell Mrs Helen Abernethie the truth and ask for her help.'

Inspector Morton smiled.

Chapter 14

Two days later, Hercule Poirot said to the Enderby Hall housemaid, 'Thank you. You have been most kind.'

Janet left the room. These foreigners, she thought! The questions they asked. It was all very well for Mrs Helen Abernethie to say that Monsieur Pontarlier was a doctor who wanted to buy the house and was also interested in unsuspected heart conditions such as the one Mr Abernethie must have had. But what business was it of his to <u>nose around</u> asking questions about the medicines the Master had taken, and where they were kept! And asking if any of the medicines he took were still in the house. Of course they had all been thrown away.

Poirot went downstairs in search of Lanscombe. It was quite clear to him that anybody could have got into the house on the day before Richard Abernethie died, and put poison into one of his medicines. Or someone could have put poison pills into the bottle next to his bed where his sleeping pills were. This was more likely.

The front door was kept locked at all times, but there was a side door that led to the garden which was not locked until the evening. At about quarter-past one, when the gardeners had gone to lunch and when the household was in the dining room or kitchen, Poirot had entered the grounds through the main gate, walked through the garden to the side door, and gone up the stairs to Richard Abernethie's bedroom without meeting anybody.

Yes, it could have been done. But the murder – if it was murder – of Richard Abernethie could never be proved. It was Cora Lansquenet's murder for which evidence was needed. What Poirot now wanted was to study the people who had been at the funeral by watching and talking to them, and then make his own conclusions about them.

'Yes, Sir?' Lanscombe said politely.

'Mrs Abernethie tells me that you had hoped to live in the cottage by the gates when you retired?'

'That is so, Sir. Naturally all that is changed now. When . . .'

Poirot interrupted, 'It might still be possible. The cottage is not needed for the U.N.A.R.C.O guests and the people who will look after them.'

'Well, thank you, Sir. Most of the guests would be foreigners, wouldn't they?'

'Yes. Amongst those who came from Europe to this country before and during the war are several who are old and unwell. The organization I work for has raised money to buy country homes for them. This place is, I think, very suitable.'

Lanscombe sighed. 'If Enderby Hall has to be sold, I'm pleased to think that it's going to be the kind of place you're talking about. We've always welcomed the unfortunate in this country, Sir; it has always been something to be proud of.'

'Thank you, Lanscombe,' said Poirot gently. 'Your Master's death must have been a great shock to you.'

'It was, Sir. No one could have had a better Master.'

'I have been talking with my friend and – er – colleague, Dr Larraby. We were wondering if your Master could have had an unpleasant interview on the day before he died? You do not remember if any visitors came to the house that day?'

'Some nuns called, collecting money for sick children – and a young man came to the back door to sell some brushes. Nobody else.'

Poirot went to see Marjorie, the cook, and had no difficulty in finding out exactly what had been served at dinner the night before Richard Abernethie had died, but he learned nothing of value from her.

He went now to get his overcoat and a couple of scarves, and went out into the garden and joined Helen Abernethie, who was cutting some flowers.

'Have you found out anything new?' she asked.

'Nothing. But I did not expect to do so. Now tell me, Madame, of those at Mr Richard Abernethie's funeral, who knew Cora best?'

'Lanscombe. He remembers her from when she was a child. The housemaid, Janet, came after Cora had married and gone away.'

'And after Lanscombe?'

Helen said thoughtfully, 'I suppose – *I* did.'

'Then why, on the day of the funeral, do you think she asked that question about Richard Abernethie being murdered?'

Helen smiled. 'It was very typical of Cora! But I never knew whether she was just innocently asking such questions – or whether she wanted to shock people.'

Poirot changed the subject. 'Mrs Maude Abernethie stayed the night after the funeral. Did she talk to you at all about what Cora had said? Did she take it seriously?'

'Oh no.'

'And you, Madame, did you take it seriously?'

Helen Abernethie said thoughtfully, 'Yes, Monsieur Poirot, I think I did.'

'Because of your feeling that something was wrong?'

'Perhaps.'

He continued, 'There had been a separation, lasting many years, between Mrs Lansquenet and her family, and then, suddenly, Richard Abernethie went to see her. Why?'

'I really don't know. He told me that he was going to see his brother Timothy, but he never mentioned Cora at all.'

As they went in by the side door, Poirot said, 'You are sure that during your visit, Richard said nothing to you about any member of the family which might be relevant?'

Helen said, 'You are speaking like a policeman.'

'I *was* a policeman – once. And you want the truth, Mr Entwhistle tells me?'

Helen said with a sigh, 'Richard was disappointed in the younger generation. But there was nothing – *nothing* – that could possibly suggest a motive for murder.'

'Ah,' said Poirot.

In the sitting room Helen began to arrange the flowers in a bowl.

'You arrange these beautifully, Madame. I think that *anything* you do, you would manage to do with perfection.'

'Thank you, Monsieur. I think this would look good on that green marble table.'

There was a bouquet of wax flowers under a glass <u>shade</u> on the table. As she lifted it off, Poirot said, 'Did anyone tell Mr Abernethie that his niece Susan's husband had almost poisoned a customer when making up a medicine? Ah!'

The shade had slipped from Helen's fingers. It dropped on the floor and broke.

'How careless of me. However, I can get a new glass shade. I'll put the flowers and the broken shade in the cupboard behind the stairs.'

It was not until Poirot had helped her to carry the pieces to the cupboard that he said, 'It was my fault. I should not have shocked you.'

'What was it that you asked me? I have forgotten.'

'Oh, there is no need to repeat my question. Indeed – I have forgotten what it was.'

Helen put her hand on his arm. 'Monsieur Poirot, is there anyone who doesn't have secrets that they would prefer stayed secret? Must these things be revealed when they have nothing to do with – with . . .'

'With the death of Cora Lansquenet? Yes. Because one has to examine *everything,* and *everyone has something to hide.* I say to you, nothing can be ignored. I am not the police and what I learn does not interest me. But I have to *know.* I need, Madame, to meet everyone who was here on the day of the funeral. And it would be much easier if I could meet them *here,* and so I have a plan. The house, Mr Entwhistle will tell the family, is to be bought by U.N.A.R.C.O., and I will be here as that organization's representative. I will call myself Monsieur Pontarlier and Mr Entwhistle will invite the family to come here and choose those things they would like before everything is sold. The young people will come easily. But the problem is that Mr Timothy Abernethie never leaves his home.'

Helen smiled. 'I believe you may be lucky there, Monsieur Poirot. I spoke to Maude yesterday. They have workmen in, painting the house and Timothy says the smell of the paint is making him ill. I think that they would be pleased to come here for a week or two. Maude is still not able to move around very well because she broke her ankle.'

'I had not heard. How unfortunate.'

'Luckily they have got Cora's companion, Miss Gilchrist, with them. She has turned out to be a huge help.'

'Did they ask for Miss Gilchrist to go to them? Who suggested it?'

'Susan fixed it up. Susan Banks.'

'Aha,' said Poirot. 'Susan likes to make arrangements. Did you hear that Miss Gilchrist was poisoned and nearly died?'

'No!' Helen looked shocked. 'Oh! Get them all here! Find out the truth! There mustn't be any more murders.'

Chapter 15

At Maude and Timothy Abernethie's house, Miss Gilchrist had hurried out to the hall to answer the telephone, which was behind the staircase.

'It's Mrs Helen Abernethie speaking,' she called up to Maude.

'Tell her I'm just coming.' Maude came down the stairs slowly because of her broken ankle.

Miss Gilchrist said quietly, 'I'm so sorry you've had to come down, Mrs Abernethie. I'll just go up and get Mr Abernethie's coffee tray.'

Timothy looked at Miss Gilchrist angrily. As she picked up the tray he asked, 'Who's that on the telephone?'

'Mrs Helen Abernethie.'

'Oh? I suppose they'll talk for an hour! Pull that curtain aside, will you? And – Where are you going?'

'It's the front doorbell, Mr Abernethie.'

'I didn't hear anything,' Timothy said as Miss Gilchrist quickly left the room. Moments later she came up to Maude Abernethie, who was still on the telephone, to say, 'I'm so sorry to interrupt. It's a nun. Collecting.'

Maude Abernethie said into the telephone, 'Just a moment, Helen,' and to Miss Gilchrist, 'I only give money to our local church.'

Miss Gilchrist hurried away again.

Maude finished her conversation and came into the front hall. Miss Gilchrist was standing completely still by the sitting room door. She jumped when Maude spoke to her.

'There's nothing the matter, is there, Miss Gilchrist?'

'Oh no, Mrs Abernethie, I was thinking about something . . .'

Maude Abernethie climbed the stairs painfully to her husband's room.

'That was Helen. Enderby Hall is definitely sold. Helen suggests that we might like to go there for a visit before it goes. She was very upset about the way the smell of the paint is affecting your health. The servants are there still, so you could be looked after comfortably.'

Timothy, who had been looking angry, now nodded his head approvingly. 'It's thoughtful of Helen,' he said. 'But moving might be too much for me.'

'Perhaps you'd prefer a hotel, dear,' said Maude. 'A good hotel is very expensive, but where your health is . . .'

Timothy interrupted. 'Maude, we *are not millionaires*. Why go to a hotel when Helen has very kindly suggested that we could go to Enderby? Not that it's really for her to suggest! And I would like to see the old place again before I die. Yes, it is an excellent plan. The painters can finish while we are away and that Gillespie woman can stay here and look after the house.'

'She's called Gilchrist,' said Maude.

Timothy waved a hand and said that it didn't matter what her name was.

★ ★ ★

'I can't do it,' said Miss Gilchrist. She was shaking. 'I simply can't stay here all alone. I've never been a nervous woman – but now I'd be terrified to be all alone here.'

'Of course,' said Maude. 'It's stupid of me – after what happened at Lytchett St Mary.'

'I suppose that it's . . . it's not logical, I know. But even that nun coming to the door startled me. Oh dear, I *am* in a bad way . . .'

Chapter 16

Hercule Poirot drank his after-dinner coffee slowly and between half-closed eyes looked at the other people in the room. He had wanted them there – all together, and he had got them. Mr Entwhistle had described all these people well but Poirot had wanted to see for himself, then he would have a very good idea – not of *how* and *when* – but of *who* would be prepared to kill.

But it was not going to be easy. He could see almost all of these people as a possible – though not a likely – murderer.

George Crossfield might kill – as a hunted animal might kill to defend itself.

Susan Banks could do it calmly – efficiently – to further a plan.

Gregory Banks could, because he had something in him which wanted punishment.

Michael Shane was possible because he was ambitious and had a murderer's <u>vanity</u>.

Rosamund Shane could, because she saw everything in the most simple way.

Timothy Abernethie could do it because he really wanted the power his brother's money would give him.

Maude Abernethie might be able because Timothy had become her child and where her child was concerned, she would be <u>ruthless</u>.

Even Miss Gilchrist, he thought, might have thought about murdering someone if it could have given her back the Willow Tree tearoom!

And Helen Abernethie? She was too civilized – too lacking in violence. And she had loved Richard Abernethie as a brother.

Poirot sighed. There would have to be more conversation. Much more conversation. For in conversation, either through a lie or through truth, people always gave themselves away.

He had been introduced by Helen to the group as Monsieur Pontarlier, a doctor, the representative of U.N.A.R.C.O. He had watched and listened – openly and behind doors! He had talked with all of them, had spent a long half-hour listening to Timothy talking about his health and the terrible effects of paint on it. Paint? Poirot frowned. Somebody else had said something about paint – Mr Entwhistle?

There had also been a discussion of a different kind of painting. Pierre Lansquenet as a painter; of Cora Lansquenet's paintings, praised by Miss Gilchrist, laughed at by Susan.

'Just like picture postcards,' she had said. 'She painted them from postcards, too.'

Miss Gilchrist had been upset and had said that dear Mrs Lansquenet always painted from nature.

'But she didn't,' said Susan to Poirot when Miss Gilchrist had gone out of the room.

'And how do you know?'

Poirot watched the confident way Susan replied.

She will always be sure, this one, he thought. And perhaps sometimes, she will be too sure . . .

Susan continued, 'One picture is of a village called Polflexan, showing the lighthouse and the pier. But the pier was destroyed in the war, and since Aunt Cora's sketch was only done two years ago, it can't really be from nature, can it? But the postcards they sell there still show the pier as it used to be. There was one in her bedroom. It's funny, isn't it, the way people get found out?'

'Yes, it is, as you say, funny.'

'I suppose you'll have to cut Enderby up and have lots of horrible small rooms.'

'In the bedrooms, yes. But most of the ground floor rooms we shall not touch. Does it sadden you, Madame, that this old family mansion of yours should go this way – to strangers?'

'Of course not.' Susan looked amused. 'I've always thought the house was ugly on the outside – and almost unacceptably luxurious inside.'

'But I understand that you yourself are planning such a place? Everything luxurious and the best that money can buy.'

Susan laughed. 'It's just a place of business. Women think a great deal about their appearance – and that's where I come in.'

'Tell me.'

And she told him about her plans for a beauty salon. He appreciated her business sense, her boldness of planning and her attention to detail. Perhaps a little ruthless . . . Watching her, he had said, 'Yes, you will succeed. How fortunate that you have the money. To have had these creative ideas and to have had no money . . . '

'I would have raised the money somehow – got someone to invest in me!'

'Ah! Of course. Even if he had not died, your uncle would have invested in you.'

'Oh no, he wouldn't. Uncle Richard made me very angry. The old shouldn't stand in the way of the young. I – oh, I beg your pardon.'

Hercule Poirot laughed easily and stroked his moustache. 'I am old, yes. But I do not stand in the way of young people. And here is your husband come to join our little discussion . . . We talk, Mr Banks, of opportunity – opportunity that must be taken with both hands. Let us hear your views.'

But Gregory Banks said nothing!

Poirot had talked with Maude Abernethie, who said how fortunate it had been that Timothy was able to come to Enderby, and how kind it had been of Helen to invite Miss Gilchrist also.

'For she is *most* useful,' Maude said. 'It was really fortunate that she was too scared to stay alone in our house, though I admit I was annoyed at the time.'

'Too scared?'

Poirot listened whilst Maude explained.

'She was frightened, you say? And yet could not exactly say why? Had anything particular happened that day?' he asked.

'Oh, I don't think so. It seems to have started when she left Lytchett St Mary, or so she said. She didn't seem to mind being alone when she was there.'

And the result, Poirot thought, had been a piece of poisoned wedding cake. Not very surprising that Miss Gilchrist was frightened after that . . . But something in Timothy Abernethie's house had made Miss Gilchrist afraid. What?

Finding himself alone with Miss Gilchrist for a few minutes before dinner, Poirot had raised the subject. 'It would be impossible for me to mention the matter of murder to members of the family. But I am fascinated. It was such a violent crime – to attack a sensitive artist in a lonely cottage. Terrible for her family. But terrible, also, for *you*. Since Mrs Maude Abernethie says that you were there at the time?'

'Yes, I was. And if you'll excuse me, Monsieur Pontarlier, I don't want to talk about it.'

'I understand completely.'

Poirot waited. And, as he had thought, Miss Gilchrist immediately began to talk about it.

'You were wise, I think, not to stay in that cottage alone,' he said when she had finished. 'I understand that you were even afraid to be alone in the house of Mr Timothy Abernethie whilst they came here?'

'I'm ashamed about that. It was just a kind of panic I had – I really don't know *why*.'

'But you had just recovered from a terrible attempt to poison you – and you are still frightened, are you not?'

'Oh, not since I came here. There are so many people and such a nice family atmosphere. Oh, no, everything seems all right here.'

'It seems to me that there must have been something that happened at Stansfield Grange, Timothy and Maude's house, that made you so afraid. I think some small happening might have made your <u>subconscious</u> fears reach a high point. Now what, do you think, was this happening?'

Miss Gilchrist thought for a moment, and then said, unexpectedly, 'I think, you know, Monsieur Pontarlier, it was the *nun*.'

Before Poirot could question this, Susan and her husband came in, closely followed by Helen.

'A nun,' thought Poirot . . . 'Now where have I heard something about a nun?'

He decided to lead the conversation on to nuns during the evening.

Chapter 17

The family's general opinion was that Helen should have avoided having Monsieur Pontarlier at Enderby Hall during this particular weekend, but fortunately this strange little foreigner did not seem to know much English.

After twenty-four hours of walking round and examining the contents of the house, the heirs of Richard Abernethie were ready to say what they wanted.

'I don't suppose I have long to live,' said Timothy in a weak voice. 'And because I loved it as a child, I would like to have the <u>Spode</u> china dinner service.'

'You're too late, Uncle,' George said. 'I asked Helen for the Spode this morning.'

Timothy became purple in the face. 'Now look here, I'm Richard's only surviving brother. That service is *mine*.'

'No Uncle, the Spode's mine. <u>First come, first served</u>.'

'<u>Nonsense</u>!' Timothy placed a hand to his heart, and groaned, 'This is very bad for me. If I could have – a little brandy.'

Miss Gilchrist hurried to get it. 'Here you are, Mr Abernethie. Please – please don't excite yourself. Are you sure you shouldn't go up to bed?'

'Don't be a fool.' Timothy drank the brandy. 'I'm not leaving this room until this is settled.'

'Really, George,' said Maude. 'If Timothy wants the Spode service, he will have it!'

'It's ugly anyway,' said Susan.

'Shut up, Susan,' said Timothy.

In a voice that was a little higher than his ordinary tones, Gregory said, 'Don't speak like that to my wife!' He half rose from his seat.

Susan said quickly, 'It's all right, Greg. I don't mind.'

'But *I* do.'

Helen said, 'George, I think it would be nice to let your uncle have the Spode.'

And George, with a slight bow to Helen said, 'Anything *you* want me to do, Aunt Helen, I will!'

'You didn't really want it, anyway, did you?' said Helen.

He laughed. 'The trouble with you, Aunt Helen, is that you see things too clearly! Don't worry, Uncle Timothy, the Spode is yours. It was just my idea of fun.'

Timothy leaned forward angrily. 'You expected that Richard would make you his heir, didn't you? But my poor brother knew where the money would go if you had control of it. You would have gambled it away. And he suspected you of being a <u>crook</u>, didn't he?'

George said quietly, 'Shouldn't you be careful about what you are saying?'

'I wasn't well enough to come here for the funeral,' said Timothy, 'but Maude told me what Cora said. Cora always was a fool – but there *may* have been something in it! And if so, I know who I'd suspect . . .'

'Timothy!' Maude stood up. 'You must think about your health. Come up with me and go straight to bed. Timothy and I, Helen, will take the Spode in memory of Richard. There is no problem, I hope?'

Nobody spoke, and she went out of the room supporting Timothy with a hand under his elbow.

Michael Shane laughed. 'You know, I'm enjoying all this! By the way, Rosamund and I want that marble table in the green sitting room.'

'Oh, no,' cried Susan. '*I* want that for my new beauty salon – and I will put a great bouquet of wax flowers on it.'

'But, darling,' said Rosamund, '*we* want it for the new play. It will be absolutely *right*.'

'I see what you mean, Rosamund,' said Susan. 'But you could easily have a painted table for the stage – it would look just the same. But for my beauty salon I've *got* to have the real thing. We will talk about it tomorrow.'

'This house is full of so many beautiful things,' Miss Gilchrist said. 'That green table would look wonderful in your new salon, I'm sure, Mrs Banks. And wax flowers do look so right on that table – really artistic and pretty.'

Greg said, speaking again in that high nervous voice, 'Susan *wants* that table.'

There was a moment of unease.

Helen said quickly, 'And what do you *really* want, George?'

George <u>grinned</u> and the tension relaxed. 'Timothy's played the poor sick man for so long that he thinks only about what *he* wants and makes sure he gets it,' said George.

'I don't believe there's anything at all the matter with him,' Susan said. 'Do you, Rosamund?'

'What?'

'Anything the matter with Uncle Timothy.'

'No – no, I don't think so.' Rosamund was lost in her own thoughts. 'I'm sorry. I was thinking about what stage lighting would be right for the table.'

'A single-minded woman,' said George. 'Your wife's dangerous, Michael. I hope you realize it.'

'I realize it,' said Michael seriously.

Helen changed the subject deliberately, turning to her foreign guest. 'I'm afraid this is all very boring for you, Monsieur Pontarlier.'

'Not at all, Madame. I think it is the greatest honour that I am allowed into your family life –' he bowed. 'I would like to say that this house will be perfect for my elderly refugees. What peace! I hear that there was also the question of a school coming here, run by "nuns", I think you say? You would have preferred that, perhaps?'

'Not at all,' said George. 'But what I do find strange is why they should all dress as if they lived hundreds of years ago!'

'And it makes them look so alike, doesn't it?' said Miss Gilchrist. 'I got so nervous when I was at Mrs Abernethie's and a nun came to the door. I thought she was the same nun who came to the door on the day of the inquest on poor Mrs Lansquenet. I felt as though she had been following me round!'

'They both had the same type of face?' Hercule Poirot asked.

'I suppose that must be it. The upper lip looked almost as though she had a moustache. Of course it was very foolish of me. I knew that afterwards.'

'A nun's costume would be a good <u>disguise</u>,' said Susan thoughtfully, 'even for a man. It hides the feet.'

'The truth is,' said George, 'you don't often look properly at anyone. That's why there are such very different descriptions of what an accused person looks like from different witnesses in court.'

'Another strange thing,' said Susan, 'is that you sometimes see yourself in a mirror unexpectedly and you say to yourself, "That's somebody I know well . . ." and then suddenly realize it's you!'

George said, 'It would be more difficult still if you could really see yourself – and not a mirror image.'

'Why?' asked Rosamund, looking puzzled.

'Because nobody ever sees themselves – *as they appear to other people.* They always see themselves in a mirror as a reversed image.'

Agatha Christie

'But why does that look any different?'

'Because people's faces aren't the same both sides. Their eyebrows are different, and their mouths go up at one side, and their noses aren't really straight.'

With a sigh, Hercule Poirot rose to his feet and said a polite good night to Helen Abernethie. 'And perhaps, Madame, I had better say goodbye. My train leaves at nine o'clock tomorrow morning. So I will thank you now for all your kindness. You will return now to your villa in Cyprus?'

'Yes.' A little smile appeared on Helen Abernethie's lips.

Poirot said, 'You are pleased, yes? You have no regrets?'

'At leaving England? Or leaving here, do you mean?'

'I meant – leaving here.' said Poirot.

'Oh – no. It's no good, is it, to hold on to the past? We must all leave that behind.'

'If we can,' Poirot said. 'Sometimes the past will not be left. It stays next to us – it says, "*I am not finished with you yet.*"'

'You mean,' said Michael, 'that your refugees when they come here will not be able to put their past completely behind them?'

'I did not mean my refugees.'

'He meant us, darling,' said Rosamund. 'He means Uncle Richard and Aunt Cora and the hatchet and all that.' She turned to Poirot. 'Didn't you?'

'Why do you think that, Madame?'

'Because you're a detective. That's why you're here. NARCO or whatever you call it, is just nonsense, isn't it?'

Chapter 18

There was a moment of great tension. Poirot said, with a little bow, 'You have great <u>insight</u>, Madame.'

'No,' said Rosamund. 'I saw you once in a restaurant. A friend told me who you were.'

'But you have not mentioned it – until now?'

'I thought it would be more fun not to,' said Rosamund.

Michael said, 'My – dear girl.'

Poirot looked at him. Michael was angry. Angry and something else – worried?

Poirot's eyes went slowly round all the faces. Susan's, angry and watchful; Gregory's, closed; Miss Gilchrist's, foolish, her mouth wide open; George's, suspicious; Helen's, upset and nervous.

He wished he could have seen their faces a second earlier, when the words 'a detective' fell from Rosamund's lips. 'Yes,' he said. 'I am a detective. I was asked to investigate Richard Abernethie's death. It would be good, would it not, if you could be certain that Richard Abernethie died a natural death?'

'Of course he died a natural death. Who says anything else?' Susan asked.

'Cora Lansquenet said so. And Cora Lansquenet is dead herself,' said Poirot.

'She said it in this room,' said Susan. 'But I didn't really think . . .'

'Didn't you, Susan?' George Crossfield said. 'Why pretend any more? You won't fool Monsieur Pontarlier!'

'We *all* thought so really,' said Rosamund. 'And his name is Hercules something.'

Poirot bowed. 'Hercule Poirot – at your service,' he said, but his name seemed to mean nothing at all to them.

'May I ask what conclusions you have come to?' asked George.

'He won't tell you, darling,' said Rosamund. 'Or if he does tell you, what he says won't be true.'

She was the only person in the room who appeared to be amused. Hercule Poirot looked at her thoughtfully.

★ ★ ★

Hercule Poirot did not sleep well that night. He was anxious, and he was not really sure *why* he was anxious. In his mind he heard bits of conversation, saw various glances, strange movements . . . Helen dropping the wax flowers when he had said – *what* was it he had said? He couldn't remember . . .

He slept then, and as he slept he dreamed of the green marble table. On it were the glass-covered wax flowers – only the whole thing had been painted over with thick, red oil paint. Paint the colour of blood and Timothy was saying, 'I'm dying – dying . . . this is the end.'

The end – a deathbed, with candles round it and a nun praying. If he could just see the nun's face, he would know.

Hercule Poirot woke up – and he did know!

Yes, it *was* the end.

Though there was still a long way to go.

★ ★ ★

Sitting in front of her dressing table, Helen Abernethie stared at herself in the mirror. What was it George had said? About seeing yourself? That day after the funeral. How had they all looked to Cora? How had Helen herself looked?

Her right – no, her *left* eyebrow was arched a little higher than the right. The shape of the mouth was the same on both sides. If she met herself, she would surely not see much difference from this mirror image. Not like Cora.

Cora, on the day of the funeral, her head tilted sideways – asking her question – looking at Helen . . .

Suddenly Helen raised her hands to her face. She said to herself, '*It doesn't make sense . . .*'

★ ★ ★

'I'm terribly sorry to get you out of bed like this,' Helen said into the phone, 'but you did tell me once to ring you up immediately if I remembered what it was that made me uneasy when Cora said that Richard had been murdered.'

'Ah! And you *have* remembered?' Mr Entwhistle said, no longer surprised at being woken at seven in the morning.

'Yes, but it doesn't make sense.'

'Was it something you noticed about one of the people?'

'Yes. It came to me when I was looking at myself in the mirror. Oh . . .'

Helen's little half cry was followed by a sound that Mr Entwhistle couldn't place at all. He said urgently, 'Hello – hello – are you there? Helen, are you there?'

Chapter 19

It was not until nearly an hour later that Mr Entwhistle found himself at last speaking to Hercule Poirot. 'Thank goodness!' said Mr Entwhistle. 'I had the greatest difficulty in getting through to Enderby.'

'That is not surprising,' said Poirot. 'The receiver was off the telephone. *Mon ami*, Helen Abernethie was found by the housemaid about twenty minutes ago, lying by the telephone in the study. She was unconscious.'

'Do you mean she was hit on the head?'

'I think so.'

'She was telephoning me at the time. I was puzzled when our conversation ended so suddenly.'

'What did she say?'

'She said to me some time ago that when Cora Lansquenet suggested her brother had been murdered, she herself had a feeling that something was wrong. Unfortunately she could not remember *why* she had that feeling.'

'And suddenly, she did remember and phoned you to tell you?'

'Yes. She said she had remembered – but that it "didn't make sense". I asked her if it was something about one of the people who was there that day, and she said, yes, she had remembered what it was when she was looking in the mirror – and that was all. We shall have to wait until she recovers consciousness before we know.'

Poirot said seriously, 'That may be never.'

'But – that's terrible, Poirot!'

'Yes. And it shows that we have to deal with someone who is either completely ruthless or so frightened that it comes to the same thing. She is being taken to a nursing home where *no one* will be allowed in to see her. But now, there is something that I want you to do. One moment.' There was a pause, then Poirot's voice spoke again. 'I had to make sure that nobody was listening. Now, you will go to Forsdyke House, a nursing home in Bury St Edmunds. Find Dr Penrith and ask him about Gregory Banks. Find out what kind of mental illness he was being treated for. And now – goodbye.'

Poirot heard the sound of the receiver being replaced at the other end, then he heard a very faint second click – and smiled to himself. Somebody here had been listening and had replaced the receiver on the telephone in the hall.

He went out there. There was no one about. He went quietly to the cupboard behind the stairs and looked inside. At that moment Lanscombe came through the service door carrying a tray. He looked surprised to see Poirot. 'Breakfast is ready in the dining room, Sir,' he said. The old butler looked white and nervous.

'*Courage*,' said Poirot. 'All will soon be well. Would it be too much trouble to bring me a cup of coffee in my bedroom?'

'Certainly, Sir. I will send Janet up with it, Sir.'

Lanscombe looked disapprovingly at Hercule Poirot's back as Poirot climbed the stairs. The detective was wearing a brightly coloured silk dressing gown.

Hercule Poirot was dressed by the time Janet brought him his coffee. As soon as she had left the room, Poirot put on his coat and hat and went quickly down the back stairs and left the house by the side door. Soon he was speaking to Mr Entwhistle from the post office.

'Pay no attention to what I asked you to do. Someone was listening. Now, to what I really want you to do . . . You must go to the house of Mr Timothy Abernethie. There is no one there but a woman by the name of Jones. You will say to Mrs Jones that you have been asked by Mr or Mrs Abernethie to fetch a particular object and take it to London.'

'And what is this object I've got to get hold of?'

Poirot told him.

'But really, Poirot, I don't see –'

'It is not necessary for *you* to see. *I* am doing the seeing. You will take it to London, to an address in Elm Park Gardens.'

Mr Entwhistle sighed, 'If we could only guess what Helen was going to tell me.'

'There is no need to guess, I *know. I know what Helen Abernethie saw when she looked in her mirror.*'

* * *

Breakfast had been an uncomfortable meal. Neither Rosamund nor Timothy had appeared, but the others were there.

'What I can't understand,' said Susan, 'is what Helen was doing telephoning at that early hour, and who she was telephoning.'

'She probably woke up feeling ill,' said Maude, 'and came down to ring up the doctor. Then <u>fainted</u> and fell.'

The door opened and Rosamund came in, frowning. 'I can't find those wax flowers,' she said. 'The ones that were standing on the marble table on the day of Uncle Richard's funeral. Lanscombe, do you know where they are?'

'Mrs Helen had an accident with them, ma'am. She was going to find a new glass shade. They are in the cupboard behind the staircase, ma'am.'

'Come with me, Michael darling. It's dark there, and I'm not going into any dark corners by myself after what happened to Aunt Helen.'

'What *do* you mean, Rosamund?' Maude demanded. 'She fainted and fell.'

Rosamund laughed. 'Don't be silly! She was hit on the head. You'll see, one by one we will be killed and the one that's left will be the murderer. But it's not going to be *me* – who's killed, I mean.'

'And why should anyone want to kill you, beautiful Rosamund?' asked George.

Rosamund opened her eyes very wide. 'Because I know too much, of course.'

'What do you know?' Maude Abernethie and Gregory Banks spoke together.

Rosamund gave her an innocent smile. 'Wouldn't you all like to know? Come on, Michael.'

Chapter 20

At eleven o'clock, Hercule Poirot called a meeting in the library. 'Please listen carefully to what I have to say. I have been a friend for many years of Mr Entwhistle's and he was very upset by some words spoken on the day of Richard Abernethie's funeral by Mrs Lansquenet and asked me to investigate.'

No one spoke.

Poirot threw back his head. '*Eh bien*, you will all be delighted to hear that as a result of my investigations – *it is my belief that Mr Abernethie died a natural death*. That is good news, is it not?'

They stared at him and in all but the eyes of one person there still seemed to be doubt and suspicion.

The exception was Timothy Abernethie. 'Of course Richard wasn't murdered,' he said angrily. 'Well, Mr whatever your name is, I'm pleased you've had the sense to come to the right conclusion, though if you ask me, Entwhistle went far beyond his duty as Richard's lawyer to get you to come nosing about here. If the family's satisfied . . .'

'But the family wasn't satisfied, Uncle Timothy,' said Rosamund. 'And what about Aunt Helen this morning?'

'Nonsense,' said Maude. 'Helen felt ill, came down and phoned the doctor, and then . . .'

'But she didn't phone the doctor,' said Rosamund. 'I asked him . . .'

Susan said sharply, 'Who *did* she phone?'

'I don't know,' said Rosamund. 'But I'm sure I can find out'

★ ★ ★

Hercule Poirot was sitting in the summerhouse. He had told everyone that he was leaving on the twelve o'clock train. There was still half an hour until then. Half an hour for someone to come to him. Perhaps more than one person.

He waited – like a cat waiting for a mouse to come out of hiding.

It was Miss Gilchrist who came first. 'Oh, Mr Pontarlier – I can't remember your other name,' she said. 'I had to come and speak to you, although I don't like doing it. I *did* listen at the door that day Mr Richard Abernethie came to see his sister and he said something like, "There's no point in talking to Timothy. He simply won't listen. But I thought I'd like to tell you, Cora. And though you've always liked to behave as if you are simple, you've got a lot of common sense. So what would *you* do about it, if you were me?"

'I couldn't hear *exactly* what Mrs Lansquenet said, but I heard the word *police* – and then Mr Abernethie said loudly, "I can't do that. Not when it's a question of *my own niece*." And then I had to run into the kitchen because something was burning, and when I got back Mr Abernethie was saying, "Even if I die an unnatural death, I don't want the police called in. You understand that, don't you, my dear girl? But now that I *know*, I shall take all possible <u>precautions</u>." And then he said he'd made a mistake over her marriage because she had been happy with her husband.'

Miss Gilchrist stopped.

Poirot said, 'I see – I see . . . Thank you, Miss Gilchrist, for coming to see me.'

★ ★ ★

Miss Gilchrist had no sooner gone before Gregory Banks came.

'At last!' he said. 'I thought that stupid woman would never go. You're wrong about everything. Richard Abernethie *was* killed. *I* killed him.'

Hercule Poirot showed no surprise. 'How?'

Gregory Banks smiled. 'It wasn't difficult for *me*. I worked out how I didn't need to be anywhere near Enderby at the time.'

'Clever,' said Poirot. 'Why did you kill him? For the money that would come to your wife?'

'No. No, of course not. I didn't marry Susan for her *money*! Abernethie thought *I* was no good! He <u>sneered</u> at me! People can't do that to me and not be punished!'

'A most successful murder,' said Poirot. 'But why give yourself away – to me?'

'Because I had to show you that you're not as clever as you think you are – and besides – besides – It was wrong, wicked . . . I must be punished . . . I must go back there – to the place of punishment.!'

Poirot studied him for a moment or two. 'How badly do you want to get away from your wife?'

Gregory's face changed. 'Why couldn't she let me alone? She's coming now – across the lawn. Tell her I've gone to the police station. To <u>confess</u>.'

★ ★ ★

Susan came in breathlessly. 'Where's Greg? I saw him.'

'Yes. He came to tell me that it was he who poisoned Richard Abernethie.'

'What absolute *nonsense*! He wasn't even near this place when Uncle Richard died!'

'Perhaps not. Where was he when Cora Lansquenet died?'

'In London. We both were.'

Hercule Poirot shook his head. 'No, no. You went to Lytchett St Mary. My inquiries say that you were there on the afternoon Cora Lansquenet died. You parked your car in the same quarry where you left it the morning of the inquest. The car was seen and the number was noted.'

Susan stared at him. 'All right. What Cora said at the funeral worried me. I decided to go and see her, and ask her what had put the idea into her head. I got there about three o'clock, knocked and rang, but there was no answer. I didn't go round to the back of the cottage. If I had, I might have seen the broken window. I went back to London without any idea there was anything wrong.'

'I know something of your husband's history,' said Poirot. 'He has a punishment <u>complex</u>.'

'You don't understand, Monsieur Poirot. Greg has never had a *chance* in life. That's why I wanted Uncle Richard's money so badly. I *knew* Greg needed to feel he was *someone*. Everything will be different now. He will have his own laboratory. No one will tell him what to do.'

'Yes, yes – you will give him everything – but you cannot give to people what they are not capable of receiving. At the end of it all, he will still be something that he does not want to be.'

'What's that?'

'*Susan's husband*. Where Gregory Banks is concerned you have no sense of right or wrong. You wanted your uncle's money – for your husband. *How badly did you want it?*'

Angrily, Susan turned and ran away.

★ ★ ★

'I thought,' said Michael Shane, 'that I'd just come and say goodbye.'

'Your wife Rosamund,' said Poirot, 'is a very unusual woman.'

Michael raised his eyebrows. 'She's lovely, I agree. But she's not known for her intelligence.'

'She will never be clever,' Poirot agreed. 'But she knows what she wants.' He sighed. 'So few people do.' Poirot placed the tips of his fingers together. 'There have been inquiries made, you know. Not only by me.'

'You mean – the police are interested? And they've been making inquiries about me?'

Poirot said quietly, 'They are interested in the movements of Mrs Lansquenet's relations on the day that she was killed.'

'That's extremely awkward. I told Rosamund that I was having lunch with Oscar Lewis on that day. Actually I went to see a woman called Sorrel Dainton – and though that's satisfactory as far as the police are concerned, Rosamund won't be pleased.'

'I see – I see – and this Miss Dainton, she will <u>confirm</u> your alibi?'

'She won't like it – but she'll do it.'

'She would do it, perhaps, even if you were *not* having an affair with her.'

'What do you mean?'

'The lady is in love with you. When they are in love, women will <u>swear</u> to what is true – and also to what is untrue.'

'Do you mean to say that you don't believe me?'

'It does not matter if *I* believe you or not. It is not *me* you have to satisfy.'

'Who then?'

Poirot smiled. 'Inspector Morton – who has just come out through the side door.'

Michael Shane turned round quickly.

Chapter 21

'I heard you were here, Monsieur Poirot,' said Inspector Morton when they were alone. 'I came over with <u>Superintendent</u> Parwell. Dr Larraby phoned him about Mrs Helen Abernethie and he's come over to make inquiries. I wanted to ask a few questions – and the people I wanted to ask seemed, very conveniently, to be all here. Did you do that?'

'Yes, I did.'

'And as a result someone hit Mrs Helen Abernethie on the head.'

'You must not blame me for that. If she had come to *me* . . . But she did not. Instead she called her lawyer in London. Now, I will ask you, my friend, to give me a few more hours, then I may be able to hand you a piece of solid evidence.'

'We certainly need it,' said Inspector Morton. 'Though we have our found out that two nuns were out collecting money and went to Mrs Lansquenet's cottage on the day *before* she was murdered. No one answered when they knocked and rang – Mrs Lansquenet was at the Abernethie funeral and Gilchrist had gone out for the day. The point is that they say they heard sighs and groans from inside the cottage. So was there someone there? And if so, who? All the Abernethie family were at the funeral.'

'These nuns, did they return at a later date to try again?'

'Actually, they did – on the day of the inquest.'

'That fits,' said Hercule Poirot. 'You will have noticed, Inspector, that the visit of the nuns was the same day that poisoned wedding cake found its way into that cottage.'

'That's a ridiculous idea!'

'My ideas are never ridiculous,' said Hercule Poirot. 'And now, *mon cher*, I must go in search of the late Richard Abernethie's niece.'

'Now be careful what you say to Mrs Banks.'

'I do not mean Mrs Banks. I mean Richard Abernethie's *other* niece.'

★ ★ ★

Poirot found Rosamund sitting on a bench by a little pool.

'I thought you'd gone,' she said. 'It's past twelve o'clock.'

'I have missed my train,' said Poirot. 'Do you know, Madame, I have been sitting in the little summerhouse hoping that you would, perhaps, visit me there?'

'Why should I? I had a lot to think about. I don't often do much thinking – it seems a waste of time. But *this* is important. I think one ought to plan one's life just as one wants it to be.'

'And that is what you are doing?'

'Well, yes . . . I was trying to make a decision about something.'

'About your husband?'

'In a way.'

Poirot waited a moment, then he said, 'Inspector Morton has just arrived. He has come to get <u>statements</u> from you all about what you were doing on the day Cora Lansquenet was murdered.'

'I see. *Alibis*,' said Rosamund cheerfully. 'That will be hell for Michael. He thinks I don't know he spent the day with that woman.'

'How did you know?'

'It was obvious from the way he said he was going to lunch with Oscar, and his face always does something strange when he tells lies.'

'How thankful I am I am not married to you, Madame! He is not, I fear, a very faithful husband?' Poirot suggested.

'No.'

'But you do not mind?'

'Well, it's fun having a husband that all the other women want to steal from you.'

Poirot was studying her. 'And suppose someone did succeed – in stealing your husband away from you?'

'They won't,' said Rosamund. 'Not now that there's Uncle Richard's money. He can finance his own shows. And he really is good. Not like me. I love acting – but I'm terrible at it, though I do look nice. No, I'm not worried about Michael any more. Because it's *my* money, you see.'

Her eyes met Poirot's.

'I think, Madame, that you must allow your cousin Susan to have the green marble table.'

Rosamund's eyes opened very wide. 'Why should I? I *want* it.'

'I know. But you – you will keep your husband. And poor Susan, she will lose hers.'

Chapter 22

The telegram came about six o'clock that evening, and then Hercule Poirot gathered his audience and began speaking. 'The puzzle is solved. Let me first, go over the various points which were brought to my attention by the excellent Mr Entwhistle.

'First, Mr Richard Abernethie dies suddenly. Secondly, after his funeral, his sister Cora Lansquenet says, "He *was* murdered, wasn't he?" Thirdly Mrs Lansquenet is killed. Then Miss Gilchrist becomes ill after eating a piece of wedding cake, which was poisoned with arsenic. That is the *next* step in the sequence.

'I have found nothing to prove that Mr Abernethie was poisoned. Equally, I have found nothing to prove that he was *not*. But Cora Lansquenet undoubtedly asked that shocking question. And undoubtedly Mrs Lansquenet was murdered. Now, the post van driver strongly believes that he did not deliver that wedding cake. If that is so, then the parcel was left by hand and though we cannot exclude a "person unknown" – we must consider those people who were able to put the parcel where it was found. Those were: Miss Gilchrist herself, of course; Susan Banks; Mr Entwhistle and Mr Guthrie, an art critic; and a nun or nuns who called to collect money.

'Miss Gilchrist did not benefit by Richard Abernethie's death and in only a very small way by the death of Mrs Lansquenet – and Miss Gilchrist was taken to hospital with arsenic poisoning.

'Susan Banks *did* benefit from Richard Abernethie's death, and in a small way from Mrs Lansquenet's. She might have believed that Miss Gilchrist had overheard a conversation between Cora Lansquenet and Richard Abernethie which referred to her. Because of that she might have decided that Miss Gilchrist must be killed. She did, after all, refuse to eat the wedding cake.

'Mr Entwhistle did *not* benefit by either of the deaths – but he *did* have considerable control over Mr Abernethie's affairs, and there could easily be some reason why Richard Abernethie should not live too long. But – you will say – if it is Mr Entwhistle who was worried, why should he come to *me*?

'And that I will answer – it is not the first time that a murderer has been too sure of himself.

'We now come to Mr Guthrie. If Mr Guthrie is really Mr Guthrie, the art critic, then that clears him. The same is true for the nun, if she is really a nun. The question is: are these people themselves, or are they somebody else?

'And there seems to be a strange – pattern – one might call it – of a nun all through this business. A nun comes to the door of Mr Timothy Abernethie's house and Miss Gilchrist believes it is the same nun she has seen at Cora's house. Also a nun, or nuns, called *here* the day before Mr Abernethie died.

'Other features of the case caught my attention: the visit of an art critic, a smell of oil paint, a picture postcard of Polflexan harbour, and finally a bouquet of wax flowers.

'It was thinking about these things that led me to the truth. Richard Abernethie died suddenly – but there would have been no reason to suspect murder if it had not been for the words said by his sister Cora at his funeral. You all believed them because Cora Lansquenet had always been famous for speaking the truth at difficult moments.

'And now I come to the question that I suddenly asked myself: *How well did you all know Cora Lansquenet?* And *Not well at all* is the answer! There were actually only three people present that day who really *knew* Cora. Lanscombe, the butler, who is old and almost blind; Mrs Maude Abernethie who had only seen her a few times round about the date of her own wedding; and

Mrs Helen Abernethie who had not seen her for over thirty years.

'So I said to myself: "Supposing it was *not* Cora Lansquenet who came to the funeral that day?"'

'Do you mean that it wasn't Aunt Cora who was murdered, but someone else?' Susan demanded.

'No, no, it was Cora Lansquenet who was murdered. *But it was not Cora Lansquenet who came to the funeral.* The woman who came that day came for one purpose only – to create in the minds of his relations the idea that Richard Abernethie had been murdered!'

'Why? What was the point of it?' Maude asked.

'*To draw attention away from the murder of Cora Lansquenet herself.* For if Cora says that Richard has been murdered, and the next day *she herself is killed*, then her death will be believed to be the result of what she said. But if Cora had simply been murdered without making her comment about Richard's death, and if the "robbery" did not convince the police, then suspicion would be likely to fall on the woman who shared the house with her.'

Miss Gilchrist protested, 'Oh really, you don't suggest I'd commit a murder for a piece of jewellery and a few worthless watercolours?'

'No,' said Poirot. 'But one of those watercolours represented Polflexan harbour which, as Mrs Banks realized, had been copied from a picture postcard which showed the old pier still in position. Yet Mrs Lansquenet painted always from life. Mr Entwhistle had mentioned there being *a smell of oil paint* in the cottage. You can paint, can't you, Miss Gilchrist? And you had been painting over another picture. You know a lot about painting. Supposing that one of the pictures that Cora bought at a sale was a really valuable one. Supposing that she did not recognize it, but that you did. You knew she was expecting a visit from a well-known art critic. Then her brother died suddenly – and a plan comes into your head. It was easy to put a sleeping drug in her morning tea that would keep her unconscious for the whole of the day of the funeral whilst you played her part at Enderby. She talked a lot about her childhood days so it was easy for you to "remember" incidents and objects. You were wearing Cora's clothes, with padding to make you look larger, and a false fringe. And Cora had certain mannerisms, all of which you had practised carefully before a mirror.

'But *you forgot that a mirror image is reversed*. When you saw in the glass the perfect reproduction of Cora's sideways movement of the head, you didn't realize that it was actually the *wrong way round*. You saw Cora tilting her head to the *right* – but your own head was tilted to the *left* to produce that effect *in the mirror*.

'That was what puzzled Helen Abernethie at the moment when you asked your famous question. Something seemed to her "wrong". I realized myself the other night when Rosamund Shane made an unexpected comment about what happens on such an occasion. Everybody looks at the *speaker*. After the talk about mirror images, I think Helen Abernethie experimented before her mirror. She probably thought of Cora, remembered how Cora used to tilt her head to the right, did so, and looked in the mirror – when, of course, she realized just what had been wrong on the day of the funeral. She was determined to tell Mr Entwhistle of her discovery as soon as she woke next morning. But someone who was used to getting up early followed her downstairs and hit her on the head.

'I may as well tell you now that Mrs Abernethie is not seriously ill. She will soon be able to tell us her own story. That aside, at any moment you were prepared to admit that you had listened to a conversation between Richard and his sister. What he actually told her, no doubt, was the fact that he had not long to live, and that explains a phrase in the letter he wrote to her after getting home. The "nun" was another of your suggestions. The nuns who called at the cottage on the day of the inquest suggested to you a mention of a nun who was "following you round", and you used that when you were anxious to hear what Maude Abernethie was saying to her sister-in-law at Enderby. And also because you wished to go with her there and find out for yourself just what suspicions there were. To poison *yourself*, badly but not <u>fatally</u>, with arsenic, is a very old trick– and made Inspector Morton suspicious of you.'

'But the picture?' said Rosamund. 'What was it?'

Poirot slowly unfolded a telegram. 'This morning Mr Entwhistle went to Mr Timothy Abernethie's house to look among the pictures in Miss Gilchrist's room. He was to take the one of Polflexan Harbour to London and go to Mr Guthrie whom I had contacted by telegram. The hastily painted sketch of Polflexan was removed from the surface and the original picture was exposed.'

He held up the telegram and read:

'*Definitely a Vermeer. Guthrie.*'

Suddenly, Miss Gilchrist spoke. 'I *knew* it was a Vermeer. *She* didn't know! She was always talking about Enderby, and what they did there as children. You don't know how boring it is, listening to somebody saying the same things, hour after hour and day after day. Boring – boring – *boring*. And nothing to look forward to. And then – a Vermeer! Another Vermeer sold recently for over five thousand pounds!'

'You killed her for five thousand pounds?' Susan's voice was shocked.

'Five thousand pounds,' said Poirot, 'would have paid for a *tearoom* . . .'

'At least,' Miss Gilchrist said, '*you* understand. I was going to call it the *Palm Tree*. And have wooden tables – and little chairs with striped red and white cushions . . .'

For a few moments, the tearoom that would never be, seemed more real than the sitting room at Enderby.

It was Inspector Morton who broke the silence by asking Miss Gilchrist to go with him.

'Oh, certainly,' she said. 'I don't want to give any trouble. After all, if I can't have the *Palm Tree*, nothing really seems to matter very much . . .'

She went out of the room with him and Susan said, her voice still shaken, 'I've never imagined a *ladylike* murderer. It's horrible . . .'

Chapter 23

'But I don't understand the connection between the wax flowers and the marble table,' said Rosamund.

They were at Helen's flat and Rosamund and Poirot were having tea with her.

'The table, no. But Miss Gilchrist said how nice the wax flowers looked on the green marble table. And *she* could not have seen them there. Because they had been broken and put away before she arrived. *So she could only have seen them when she was there as Cora Lansquenet.*'

'That *was* stupid of her, wasn't it?' said Rosamund.

Poirot shook a finger at her. 'It shows you, Madame, the dangers of *conversations*. It is a strong belief of mine that if you can get a person to talk to you for long enough, *on any subject whatever* – sooner or later they will give themselves away. Miss Gilchrist did.'

'I shall have to be careful,' said Rosamund thoughtfully. 'Did you know? I'm going to have a baby. And I've decided to leave the stage and just be a mother. Michael is *delighted*. I didn't really think he would be. So Susan's got the marble table. I thought, as I was having a baby . . .'

She left the sentence unfinished.

'I think Susan is going to have a big success with her beauty business,' said Helen.

'Yes, she was born to succeed,' said Poirot.

'Greg's gone away somewhere,' said Rosamund. 'He's having a rest cure, Susan *says*.'

Poirot turned to Helen. 'And you, Madame, are off to Cyprus?'

'Yes, in two weeks.'

'Then let me wish you a happy journey.'

She went with him to the door, and said, 'Monsieur Poirot, the income Richard left me meant more to me than theirs did to any of the others. You see – there is a child in Cyprus . . . After my husband died, my loneliness was unbelievable and when I was nursing in London at the end of the war, I met someone . . . We lived together for a little while, then he went back to Canada – to his wife and his children. He never knew about – our child. It seemed like a miracle to me – a middle-aged woman with everything seemingly behind her. Now, with Richard's money, I can send my "nephew" to an even better school, and give him a start in life. I never told Richard. He was fond of me – but he would not have understood. I wanted you to know this about me.'

Poirot bowed over her hand.

★ ★ ★

He got home to find someone sitting in the armchair on the left of the fireplace.

'Hello, Poirot,' said Mr Entwhistle. 'I've just come back from the trial. They brought in a verdict of guilty, of course. But Miss Gilchrist is happy, you know. She spends most of her time making plans to run a chain of tearooms.'

'Some people might think that she was always a little mad,' said Poirot. 'But me, I think not.'

'Goodness me, no, Poirot! She was as sane as you and I when she planned Cora's murder and carried it out <u>in cold blood</u>.'

Poirot gave a little shiver. 'I am thinking,' he said, 'of some words that Susan Banks said – that she had never imagined a *ladylike* murderer.'

'Why not?' said Mr Entwhistle. 'It takes all sorts.'

They were silent – and Poirot thought of murderers he had known.

CHARACTER LIST

(Please see the Abernethie family tree on page vi for other family members)

Lanscombe: butler to Mr Richard Abernethie at Enderby Hall

Richard Abernethie: a wealthy businessman who has just died

Mortimer Abernethie: adult son of Richard who died six months before his father's death

Timothy Abernethie: a younger brother of Richard; still alive

Cora Lansquenet: the youngest sister of Richard; no children. Her husband, now dead, was Pierre Lansquenet, a painter.

Mr Entwhistle: the Abernethie family lawyer

Helen Abernethie: the widow of Leo, Richard Abernethie's dead brother; no children

George Crossfield: the son of Laura Abernethie; a lawyer

Maude Abernethie: the wife of Timothy, Richard Abernethie's brother

Rosamund Shane: the daughter of Geraldine, Richard Abernethie's dead sister; married to Michael Shane

Michael Shane: Rosamund's husband, an actor

Susan Banks: the daughter of Gordon Abernethie, now dead

Gregory (Greg) Banks: Susan's husband, a pharmacist's assistant

Miss Gilchrist: the paid companion to Cora

Detective Inspector Morton: a police officer with responsibility for investigations in the area of Lytchett St Mary

Dr Barton: Timothy's doctor

Hercule Poirot: a Belgian private detective, now retired, who has lived for many years in Britain

Georges: Poirot's manservant

Dr Larraby: Richard Abernethie's doctor before his death

Alexander Guthrie: an art critic and old friend of Cora

Dr Proctor: the village doctor in Lytchett St Mary

Andrews: the driver of the post van

Mr Goby: a private investigator for the very rich

Sorrel Dainton: an actress friend of Michael Shane

Mr Rosenheim: a theatrical colleague of the Shanes

Oscar Lewis: also a colleague of the Shanes

Monsieur Pontarlier: a name used by Poirot when visiting Enderby Hall

Superintendent Parwell: the senior policeman in the Enderby Hall area

Marjorie: the cook at Enderby Hall

Janet: the housemaid at Enderby Hall

Mrs Jones: a daily servant at Timothy and Maude Abernethie's home

CULTURAL NOTES

Wills and inheritance

A will is a legal document that describes how the money and property that someone leaves when they die is to be distributed to relatives and other people. It wasn't unusual for servants, like the old butler Lanscombe, to receive a sum of money to thank them for their loyal service. Wills were usually made in a solicitor's office but not always. To be legal, the signing of the will had to be witnessed, i.e. seen, by two people (usually not relatives) who knew the person writing the will. In addition to the two witnesses there had to be an executor. The executor was the person chosen by the person making the will to make sure that their wishes were carried out properly. Quite often the solicitor would be named as the executor, but it wasn't unusual for a family member, like Timothy, Richard Abernethie's brother, to be named.

Tearooms

Today's coffee shop or café, selling Italian or American coffee and pastries, had not, at the time of the story (early 1950s), come to Britain. Tearooms, however, were very common everywhere. People would go to them to drink good quality tea and eat homemade cakes, sandwiches and scones. They were highly respectable places and the customers were usually middle and upper class women who had been out shopping. Before the war, a lot of the food people ate in Britain was sent in from other countries by ship. When the war started, this was no longer possible because the boats that usually brought the food were attacked and destroyed and the food did not arrive.

The government had to make sure that there was enough food, not only for the people in Britain, but also for the soldiers fighting in the war. They did this by controlling how much food each person could buy every week. This was called rationing and most items of food, for example, meat, butter, eggs, tea, biscuits, fruit, sugar and chocolate were rationed. Food rationing lasted until 1954.

Inquests

If a death has been caused by anything other than natural causes, for example, a heart attack or long illness (as with Richard Abernethie) an inquest must be held. This is a public inquiry with a jury of twelve ordinary people, and a coroner, who is in charge at the inquest. Everybody, including members of the public, listen to the evidence. The jury then give their verdict and say what the cause of death was, for example, natural death, accidental death, suicide or murder. In the case of murder, a police investigation then takes place.

Post mortems, autopsies

In the UK, when a person dies, a doctor has to certify the cause of death. If the doctor does not know exactly why the person died, and the death was sudden and rather suspicious, they have to do a post mortem, also called an autopsy. This is a medical examination done by a doctor called a pathologist, who removes the internal organs of the dead person and examines them to discover the cause of death. When Richard Abernethie died, it was decided that an autopsy was unnecessary because he had been ill. Later when there was some doubt about the cause of his death, an autopsy was impossible because his body had been cremated (see Glossary). With the murder of one of Richard's relatives later in the story, an autopsy was again not done because the cause of death was obvious – the victim had been violently attacked.

Monsieur Poirot

Poirot is from Belgium and his first language is French, not English. His language is quite formal, which makes it sound 'foreign' to a native speaker. Sometimes Poirot says things that are not completely correct. The word order he uses may be wrong or he may use a word wrongly, for example, he may say *good* when he should have said *well* or the other way round. He often uses little French expressions like *mon ami* (my friend) or *Eh bien* (Oh well).

Wedding cake

At the time of the story, if you had been invited to a wedding but were unable to attend, it was usual for the couple getting married to send you a piece of their wedding cake in a small box.

Trust fund

A trust fund is an amount of money that belongs to someone but is managed by someone else, for example, if the person is too young or they are not considered responsible or knowledgeable enough to take care of it themselves. Quite often the money is invested and the person who owns it only receives the profits or interest, leaving the original amount safe. It is common for a solicitor to be the person who controls a trust fund. In the story, Richard's nephew George, who is a solicitor, is suspected of using money from his clients' trust funds to gamble with at the horse races.

Refugees

Refugees are people who have to leave their countries because of their political or religious beliefs. At the time this story was written, there were many refugees in Britain. Some were Jews who had left Eastern Europe during or before the Second World War, others had come as a result of the expansion of Communism in Eastern Europe after the war. Nobody would have thought it unusual for someone like Poirot to be representing an organization that helped refugees.

Vermeer

Johan Vermeer was a Dutch painter who lived and worked in the seventeenth century (1632–1675) although his paintings did not become valuable until the nineteenth century. Thirty-four paintings have been identified as being his work although he is actually believed to have painted sixty-six. At the time of the story, it was quite possible that a previously unknown painting by Vermeer could be discovered. It would have been very valuable.

GLOSSARY

Key

n = noun

v = verb

phr v = phrasal verb

adj = adjective

adv = adverb

excl = exclamation

exp = expression

admit (v)

to agree that something bad or embarrassing is true

affair (n)

a sexual relationship between two people who are married, but not to each other

alibi (n)

proof that you were somewhere else when a crime was committed, showing why you can't be guilty of the crime

allowance (n)

money that is given regularly to someone

ambition (n)

the desire to be successful, rich, or powerful

arsenic (n)

a very powerful poison

awkward (adj)

embarrassing and difficult to deal with – an awkward person feels uncomfortable or clumsy

beauty salon (n)
a place where you can go to have treatments for your skin, hair and nails

beneficiary (n)
someone who **inherits** money

broke (adj)
not having any money

bury (v)
when the body of a dead person is put into a grave and covered with earth

butler (n)
the most important male servant in a wealthy house

case (n)
a crime or mystery that the police are investigating

chauffeur-driven (adj)
driven by a professional driver, who often wears a uniform

client (n)
someone for whom a professional person or organization provides a service or work

coincidence (n)
when two or more similar or related events occur at the same time by chance

companion (n)
when Agatha Christie was writing, a companion was usually someone who was paid to spend time with you

complex (n)
a mental or emotional problem, often caused by an unpleasant experience in the past

confess (v)
to **admit** doing something that is wrong or that you are ashamed of

confidential (adj)
spoken or written in secret and needing to stay secret

confirm (v)
to show that what you believe is definitely true

cremate (v)
when the body of a dead person is burned, usually as part of a **funeral** service

crook (n)
a dishonest person

custom (n)
something which is usual or traditional in a particular society or in particular circumstances

Daimler (n)
an expensive car

defeat (v)
a task or a problem defeats you when it is so difficult that you cannot solve it

deliberately (adv)
doing something because you mean to do it and not by accident

deny (v)
to say that something is not true

dependent on (adj)
needing something or someone in order to succeed or be able to survive

deposit (n)
a sum of money which is part of a payment for something, or as security when you rent something

desperation (n)
the feeling that you are in such a bad situation that you will try anything to change it

disguise (n)
if you are in disguise or wearing a disguise, you have changed your appearance so that people will not recognize you

dreadfully (adv)
extremely

eh bien (exp)
French for 'Oh well' (see Cultural notes: Monsieur Poirot)

estate (n)
all the money and property someone leaves when they die

evidence (n)
information from documents, objects, or **witnesses**, which is used in a court of law to try to **prove** something

executor (n)
a person who is responsible for making sure that a dead person's instructions are carried out properly

expenses (n)
the money you spend while doing something in the course of your work, which will be paid back to you afterwards

faint (v)
to lose consciousness for a short time

fatally (adv)
causing death

fee (n)
the money that someone receives for a job or service

fellow (n)
a man

first come, first served (exp)
used when there is not enough of something for everyone, to say that the person who asks for it first will get it

flamboyantly (adv)
doing something in a stylish way that is noticeable

forbid (v)
to say that something must not be done

fortune (n)
a very large amount of money

fringe (n)
hair which is cut so that it hangs over your forehead

frown (v)
to move your eyebrows together because you are annoyed, worried, or thinking

funeral (n)
the ceremony that is held when someone has died

gamble (v)
to bet money on the result of a game, a race, or competition

generation (n)
all the people in a group or country who are of a similar age

generosity (n)
the quality of wanting to give people your money or time

grin (v)
to smile widely

groan (n)
a long, low sound of pain or unhappiness

hatchet (n)
a small axe – usually used to chop up wood

have your eye on something (exp)
to see something that you want and that you intend to get

heir (n)
someone who has the right to **inherit** a person's money, property, or title when that person dies

hesitate (v)
to pause slightly, usually because you are uncertain, embarrassed, or worried about doing something

horse-race (n)
an event where horses run races and people **gamble** on which one is going to win

hypochondriac (n)
a person who always thinks they are ill, when in reality they are not

icing (n)
a sweet substance made from powdered sugar that is used to cover and decorate cakes

in cold blood (adv)
doing something without showing pity or emotion

in debt (exp)
owing someone money

income (n)
the money that a person or organization earns or receives

indignant (adj)
being shocked and angry, because you think that something is not fair

inherit (v)
to receive money or property from someone who has died

inheritance (n)
money or property which you receive from someone who has died

inquest (n)
a meeting where **evidence** is heard about someone's death to find out
why they died (see Cultural notes)

insane (adj)
being mentally ill and not being able to behave normally and reasonably

insight (n)
the understanding of what a situation or person is really like

Inspector (n)
an officer in the British police

invalid (n)
a person who is ill or disabled and needs to be cared for by someone else

invest (v)
to use money in a way that you hope will increase its value, for example
by buying shares or property

it takes all sorts (exp)
an expression that means you think someone or their behaviour is strange

jury (n)
the group of people who have been chosen from the general public to listen to the facts about a crime and decide whether the person accused is guilty or not

late (adj)
used to talk about someone who is dead

legacy (n)
money or property which someone leaves to you in their **will** when they die

lethal dose (n)
the amount of a drug that is enough to cause death

make-believe (n)
something that you pretend is true or real

mannerism (n)
something that a person does that is typical of them

Master (n)
an old-fashioned word for the man that a servant works for

mistaken (adj)
being wrong about something

mon ami (exp)
French for 'my friend' (see Cultural notes: Monsieur Poirot)

mon cher (exp)
French for 'my dear' (see Cultural notes: Monsieur Poirot)

morphia (n)
an old-fashioned word for morphine, a very strong drug used for stopping pain

motive (n)
the reason for doing something

naïve (adj)
lacking experience and expecting things to be easy, or people to be honest or kind when they are not

nonsense (n)
something that you think is untrue or silly

nose around (phr v)
to look around somewhere because you want to try to find something

nun (n)
a female member of a religious community

nursing home (n)
a small, private hospital

old maid (n)
used impolitely to describe a woman who has never married and is not young any more

orphanage (n)
a place where orphans (children without parents) are looked after

pâté de foie gras (n)
an expensive French food made from the liver of a fattened goose

pier (n)
a large platform which sticks out into the sea and which people can walk along

place a bet (v)
to risk money on the result of a race or game in order to win more money

port (n)
a strong, sweet wine that is usually drunk after dinner

praise (v)
to express approval for a person's qualities and/or achievements

precaution (n)
an action that is intended to prevent something dangerous or unpleasant from happening

prosecution (n)
when someone is taken to court for doing something illegal

protest (v)
to complain loudly

prove (v)
to show that something is definitely true

pub (n)
a building where people can buy and drink alcoholic drinks

put something in store (exp)
putting the things that you don't use in a place so that when you want them, you can get them

quarry (n)
an area that is dug out from a piece of land or mountainside in order to get stone or minerals from it

refugee (n)
a person who has been forced to leave their country because of their political or religious beliefs

resent (v)
to feel bitter and angry

residence (n)
a formal word for the place where you live

resign (v)
to say formally that you are leaving your job

ridiculous (adj)
foolish or silly

rumour (n)
a story or piece of information that may or may not be true

ruthless (adj)
doing anything that is necessary to get what you want

sack (v)
if your employers sack you from your job, they tell you that you can no longer work for them

scone (n)
a small, round cake usually eaten with butter and jam or honey

senile (adj)
when old people become confused and are unable to look after themselves

sentimental (adj)
something that is sentimental makes you feel emotions such as love or sadness, especially for things in the past

set a trap (exp)
to trick someone so that they do or say something that catches them

shade (n)
a decorative cover

sharply (adv)
doing something in a disapproving, unfriendly or sudden way

show off (phr v)
to try to impress people by showing in a very obvious way what you can do or what you own

shudder (n)
the movement you make when you shake with fear or disgust

sinister (adj)
evil or harmful

sneer (v)
to show that you disrespect someone by what you say or by the expression on your face

snoop (v)
to secretly look around somewhere to find out things

Spode (n)
china – plates and cups – made by the company Spode are expensive and good quality

statement (n)
something that you say or write which gives information in a formal way

subconscious (n)
the part of your mind that can influence you even though you are not aware of it

Superintendent (n)
a high-ranking police officer

suspect (n)
a person who the police think may be guilty of a crime

suspect (v)
to believe that something dishonest or unpleasant has been done

suspicious (adj)
something about a person which makes you think that they are involved in a crime or a dishonest activity

swear (v)
to state that you are telling the truth

take someone into your confidence (exp)
to tell someone your secrets or the truth about something

telegram (n)
a message that is sent by telegraph and then printed and delivered to someone's home or office

testify (v)
to give a **statement** of what you saw someone do or what you know of a situation, after having promised to tell the truth

threaten (v)
to say you will harm or hurt someone, in order to get them to do what you want

tilt (v)
to move something so that it is on one side

trust fund (n)
money that is kept for someone and is used to make more money by **investing** it

uneasy (adj)
feeling that something is wrong

unwillingly (adv)
doing something without wanting to

vanity (n)
the feeling that you are very good at something

verdict (n)
a decision made in a court of law, given by the judge or **jury** at the end of a trial

Victorian (adj)
during the reign of Queen Victoria (1837–1901)

warily (adv)
doing something cautiously because you believe there may be danger or problems

widow (n)
a woman whose husband has died

will (n)
a document where you say what you want to happen to your money and property when you die (see Cultural notes)

witness (n)
a person who sees an accident or crime

wreath (n)
a ring of flowers and leaves that is put on a grave as a sign of remembrance for a dead person

yard (n)
a unit of length equal to 36 inches or approximately 91.4 centimetres

COLLINS ENGLISH READERS

THE AGATHA CHRISTIE SERIES

The Mysterious Affair at Styles
The Man in the Brown Suit
The Murder of Roger Ackroyd
The Murder at the Vicarage
Peril at End House
Why Didn't They Ask Evans?
Death in the Clouds
Appointment with Death
N or M?
The Moving Finger
Sparkling Cyanide
Crooked House
They Came to Baghdad
They Do It With Mirrors
A Pocket Full of Rye
After the Funeral
Destination Unknown
Hickory Dickory Dock
4.50 From Paddington
Cat Among the Pigeons

Visit **www.collinselt.com/agathachristie** for language
activities and teacher's notes based on this story.